SCOTT MALTHOUSE

Illustrated by BRAINBUG DESIGN

THE TERROR BENEATH

An INVESTIGATIVE ROLEPLAYING GAME
of WEIRD FOLK HORROR

OSPREY GAMES

OSPREY GAMES
Bloomsbury Publishing Plc
Kemp House, Chawley Park, Cumnor Hill, Oxford OX2 9PH, UK
29 Earlsfort Terrace, Dublin 2, Ireland
1385 Broadway, 5th Floor, New York, NY 10018, USA
E-mail: info@ospreygames.co.uk
www.ospreygames.co.uk

OSPREY GAMES is a trademark of Osprey Publishing Ltd

First published in Great Britain in 2024

A catalogue record for this book is available from the British Library.

ISBN: HB 9781472858399; eBook 9781472858405; ePDF 9781472858382; XML 9781472858375

24 25 26 27 28   10 9 8 7 6 5 4 3 2 1

Design & Layout by Dídac Gurguí
Printed and bound in India by Replika Press Private Ltd.

Osprey Games supports the Woodland Trust, the UK's leading woodland conservation charity.

To find out more about our authors and books visit www.ospreypublishing.com. Here you will find extracts, author interviews, details of forthcoming events and the option to sign up for our newsletter.

CONTENTS

THE UNKNOWN WORLD

There are sacraments of evil as well as of good about us, and we live and move to my belief in an unknown world, a place where there are caves and shadows and dwellers in twilight.

The Red Hand

The icy limbs of a spectral fog creep through the gloomy London streets. The muffled din of something they're calling 'jazz' feeds the night from cigarette-choked Soho bars. A figure fades away from the glow of street lamps, descending on an unwitting vagrant slumbering in an alley, the shadows concealing the stranger's crooked horns.

An affable young drunk staggers from Solomon's, a serpentine flapper hanging from his arm. After he stumbles into his flat his body begins to change, bulbous mushrooms erupting from his flesh, his legs becoming rooted to the floorboards. The flapper strikes his name from a crumpled list.

In the dank cellar beneath the bar, a dishevelled professor finishes his latest work: conjuring an ancient pagan god into the mind of his student through a mixture of brain surgery and magical incantation. The student awakens with eyes gleaming like emeralds.

A world away in the wilds of Caerleon, Wales, squat creatures from another age dance a malevolent ritual at their stone altar. A little girl in a white dress stumbles into a new part of the forest she's never seen before where nymphs entice her to join their strange games. She returns home to her panicked family a day later having aged 15 years.

A wounded soldier seeking respite in the hills finds a tablet etched with an unfamiliar language. Over time his wounds heal but a black pyramid haunts his dreams. He wakes in a sweat on the cool grass, staring up at the stone monument he unknowingly created and the sacrifice he's brought for them.

There are terrors lurking beneath this land. Old powers forgotten in the depths of time, lost to ancient stone etchings and stories told by the burning hearth as the gloom sets in. Dolmens haunted by the whispers of dead kings, treacherous wee folk stealing infants in the night and watching over all of it a pantheon of pagan gods gladly gorging on sacrifices of blood and gold.

But beliefs changed. As the smoke of industry darkened our skies, the gods and monsters who once walked among us retreated: into the shadows of our hillsides and beyond the Veil of the Otherworld. Depictions of the once-dangerous beings who crawled among the trees, rivers and mountains lost their teeth, becoming sweet bedtime tales.

On occasion, the unseen would become seen once more. An unlucky rambler taken by claw and tooth down into cold mountain caverns. A little boy out past his bedtime happening upon the gyrating bodies of witches by moonlight. An archaeologist chased down by a black hound, his remains never found.

Yet there were some who never forgot the old ways, and others who sought to use new technology to harness the power of the gods for their own selfish ends. As millions perished on the blood-drenched battlefields in the War to End All Wars, technological progress forged onwards at a rapid pace. Feats once thought impossible were now in the grasp of scientists and warmongers alike, with unholy experiments conducted out of sight of the world at large. The gods and monsters were once again called upon by humanity, not in service but to serve. But the hubris of man only led down the road to corruption. Playing with such powers is a fool's game and those who did so brought about a grave danger to all of civilisation. The old gods have returned: and they are wrathful.

WEIRD FOLK HORROR INVESTIGATIONS

In *The Terror Beneath*, players take on the role of occult investigators operating in Great Britain, broadly between the years 1919 and 1929: the so-called Golden Age, where Bright Young Things threw debauched parties and Hollywood films invaded the picture houses. The investigators are members of the London-based Gold Tiberius Society, whose objective is to uncover and stop the ancient evils that have stirred in the shadow of the Great War: secret societies communing with unknowable pagan gods, bloodthirsty beings from folklore emerging from the earth into an industrial civilisation, and rogue scientists blending occult knowledge and post-war technology to look beyond the curtain of reality into a realm inhabited by dread creatures lost to myth.

The Terror Beneath is a roleplaying game based on the works of master horror author Arthur Machen, whose stories such as *The Great God Pan*, The White People and *The Inmost Light* deal with themes of decadence, degeneration of the human soul and scientists meddling with occult evils. In some of Machen's best-known works his characters investigate weird occurrences in both London and the wilds of Wales where the author was born. In the same way, characters in *The Terror Beneath* move between the smog-choked city of London to the eerie pagan Welsh countryside on the trail of sinister forces from beneath the world and beyond the Veil. An investigation scenario in this game is known as a mystery.

These are just some of the mysteries that can be played out in *The Terror Beneath*:

- A chemist and member of a witch cult has manufactured a pill that transforms people into sentient oozes who collect together in the London Underground, forming an undulating mass that lures victims into the tunnels to devour. The investigators begin to find patterns around disappearances in Knightsbridge after a prominent Member of Parliament goes missing.
- A rambler in rural Caerleon is found torn apart by a Stone Age knife, an eye carved onto his chest. Residents of a nearby village fear the 'little people' of the hills, making human offerings in an attempt to appease them. The further the investigators dig, the more details they unearth of a covert military experiment designed to draw out the 'little people' and test their fighting capabilities, to be used should a new world war happen.
- In a club that doesn't officially exist, an exotic mushroom called 'the flesh of the gods' is served for dinner. Those who

eat it are each visited by a horned entity in their dreams, who compels them to burn the homes of London's most wealthy. After several similar fires, the investigators find clues that lead to the Lost Club and its enigmatic owner who may not be of this world.

- A soldier living near Wentwood, Monmouthshire, finds a well in a crumbling Roman temple that, when drank, quells the nightmares of trench warfare. Word begins to spread and soon many ex-soldiers drink from the well. But each night they sleepwalk into the woods and begin building a clay pyramid. During waking hours their words become monosyllabic and eventually they begin to speak the ancient black speech. Should they finish the pyramid, the great spider of the Otherworld, the jeelo, will emerge into the mortal world.

- The investigators are invited to an exhibit at the British Museum showcasing a perfectly preserved hunched humanoid the curator calls the 'missing link' between apes and humans. The curator is later found ritualistically slain and the exhibit is nowhere to be found. His colleague, a member of the Society of Pan, is using human blood to resurrect the 'fair folk' body, but accidentally summons a dhol worm into the belly of the museum where it must be destroyed before it can emerge onto the streets of London.

- A Hollywood actress staying at the Ritz has a strange entourage of silent men who do everything she says. In fact, she seems to have a hold over anyone she crosses paths with.

WHAT IS A ROLEPLAYING GAME?

Tabletop roleplaying games, often shortened to TTRPGs, are social games where each participant adds to an overall narrative, taking control of characters in a shared world. If you remember those choose-your-own-adventure books or have played an interactive movie on a streaming service, it's easy to imagine how a roleplaying game works. Each player takes on the role of a character who inhabits the world, while one player becomes the Game Moderator (GM).

Player Characters (PCs) are created through a set of rules to determine how well they can carry out certain actions in the game world. In *The Terror Beneath* they could be a knowledgeable curator, a curious journalist, a worldly rambler or any number of character types suitable to the era. It's the GM's job to guide the PCs through the game by presenting challenges to overcome, people to interact with and to adjudicate the rules in their fairest (and most fun) way. The GM brings the world to life through description, whether conjuring a bustling metropolis, detailing an actress' transatlantic accent or explaining how an unnatural darkness is enveloping the PCs.

It might initially seem like the GM has a pretty stressful job to do, but this shouldn't be the case and there will be more advice later in this book to help GMs in their role. The most important part of any TTRPG is that everyone is having fun.

If you want a good idea of how a TTRPG works, there are now thousands of videos online of groups playing their games for all to see, from small home games to lavishly-produced shows starring professional voice actors.

THIS GAME

At its most basic, *The Terror Beneath* is an exciting investigative roleplaying game where your characters collect clues in order to unravel occult mysteries and hopefully save the day by catching the culprit or preventing further harm. Because investigative games require a specific structure, this game uses Pelgrane Press' GUMSHOE System to emulate the fun of solving a mystery without actually needing the mind of Sherlock Holmes to do so. It's never interesting to fail a die roll when gathering information or searching for a clue, which is why GUMSHOE allows your character to gain this knowledge automatically when using relevant abilities. Rather than hitting a brick wall from a bad roll and wondering where to go next, this system allows investigators to unfurl a tapestry of clues leading to the final mystery.

The Terror Beneath specifically uses the QuickShock variation of the GUMSHOE rules to simulate the weird horror fiction of Arthur Machen. QuickShock is a simpler version of the ruleset that uses cards to represent the physical wounds and mental strain PCs will face during their investigations.

• • •

RULES IN BRIEF

In *The Terror Beneath*, each character has a combination of abilities categorised into Investigative abilities and General abilities. When creating your character, a number rating will be assigned to each ability that shows how proficient they are at certain tasks.

When using an Investigative ability, they will always gain the information they need so long as they're using a relevant ability.

Certain situations where success or failure could lead to an interesting narrative will call for the use of a General ability. This requires a test that involves rolling a six-sided die (d6) and assigning points from the relevant General ability pool. Both numbers are totalled and compared to the Difficulty number of the task. If the result meets or exceeds the Difficulty number, the character succeeds in using that ability. The maximum number that can be assigned is based on your ability rating. The margin between the result of a test and the Difficulty number can matter.

Characters can choose to spend Pushes to gain more information when using an Investigative ability.

During a fight players choose their goal, whether it's to get an item, subdue an enemy, escape or something else. Their Fighting ability is rolled against a set Difficulty based on the goal, with the margin between the Difficulty and rolls playing a key role in determining the outcome of the fight. If they succeed, they pay Tolls from a combination of their Fighting, Health and Athletics General abilities. If they don't want to pay a Toll or cannot, they may take a Minor Injury card. On a failure, Injury and Shock cards are given to players to represent physical wounds, mental traumas and emotional changes to the characters.

• • •

MATERIALS NEEDED TO PLAY

To play *The Terror Beneath*, each player should have a six-sided die (d6), a character sheet, some paper for making notes during an investigation, and something to do said writing with. The GM might find it useful to keep scenes on a set of notecards so they can lay them out as the PCs enter new locations. However, the game really shines with the use of props. This can be a fair amount of up-front work for the GM but it's worth it for a truly immersive experience. Some examples are:

• A 'stone' tablet made of clay.
• An old matchbook with notes scrawled on.
• Telegram paper.
• An old map complete with a secret message.
• A dusty book of the occult.
• Weathered luggage tags.
• Store-bought (or homemade) slime.

THE WEIRD FOLK HORROR OF ARTHUR MACHEN

While Arthur Machen, born Arthur Llewellyn Jones, isn't the most remembered horror master, he was one of the most prolific and influential of his time, penning a range of tales from the late nineteenth century to the early 1930s. He would weave his experience of growing up in Caerleon, Wales, and moving to London into his stories, bemoaning the proliferation of industry while leaning on his Christian beliefs and fascination in paganism to conjure the old terrors and numinous wonders for which he is most famed.

Probably his most famous and controversial story was *The Great God Pan*, a tale that perfectly captures the essence of weird folk horror. A precursor to Lovecraft's cosmic horror, *The Great God Pan* tells the story of a scientist who experiments on a young woman in order to lift the veil of reality from her eyes so she can view an ancient, mystical

Otherworld. The experiment goes awry and the poor girl emerges having lost her faculties, but plainly terrified of what she has experienced: coming into contact with a pagan god. Some years later, a man called Villiers is on the trail of a beautiful and terrible woman called Helen Vaughan who is driving male members of the aristocracy to suicide. As the story unfolds, we begin to understand the true nature of this woman, if a woman she was, and her sinister origin.

The Great God Pan caused outcry when it was published in 1894, with one critic remarking: '*The Great God Pan* is, I have no hesitation in saying, a perfectly abominable story, in which the author has spared no endeavour to suggest loathsomeness and horror which he describes as beyond the reach of words.'

In the same year Machen would publish *The Inmost Light*, another horror piece, this time about a scientist who transfers his wife's soul into a gem, only to have an evil presence inhabit her body in place of her soul. This theme of science converging with mysticism would again surface in *The Novel of the White Powder*, part of a renowned collection called *The Three Imposters*. Here a work-obsessed lawyer begins taking a drug that slowly changes him; first by unshackling him from his workaholic nature and later by causing him to begin rotting right in front of his sister. The ending reveals that this infernal new prescription was linked with a devil-worshipping witch cult, neatly tying together Machen's favourite themes of pagan horror, mad science and the infestation of the soul.

While many of the stories were set in London, where Machen had transplanted to chase his dreams of being an author, others returned to his homeland of Wales, dealing with beings thought dead to the annals of folklore. His so-called 'little people' stories such as *The Novel of the Black Seal* (highly influential on Lovecraft, particularly in *The Dunwich Horror*) and *The Shining Pyramid*, dealt with the hidden evils lurking in rural Wales. Machen took the folktales of fairies and gave them a particularly unpleasant origin, supposing that the 'wee folk' spoken of in ancient days were actually squat murderous creatures who still existed in the hills and barrows of Wales. We even get to witness a 'little people' mystery in the heart of London in *The Red Hand*, a story involving Machen's recurring occult investigator Dyson and his friend Phillipps.

Perhaps one of his most unsettling and influential stories was published in 1904: *The White People*. This much-anthologised novella is formed of passages from a young girl's diary as she is initiated into a world of pagan magic by her nurse, discovering a world beyond our own inhabited by strange nymphs and other alien beings whose languages and customs she learns on her journey. We see this bizarre world through the girl's eyes and it's only when we step back do we understand the true horror of the story. *The White People* would go on to influence film-maker Guillermo del Toro in *Pan's Labyrinth*.

Machen would publish fewer horror stories as the decades went by, with *The Terror* (unexplained murders occur during the Great War caused by the animal kingdom) and *Out of the Earth* (the 'little people' begin emulating the war) being two that harkened back to his weird folk horror roots.

The writer's work still ripples through pop culture, whether in the novels of Stephen King and Clive Barker, the music of The Fall and Belbury Poly or glimpsed on screen in films such as *The Ritual* and *Don't Be Afraid of the Dark*. Furthermore, his vision of an ancient evil beneath the surface attempting to scratch its way into our world, of science gone awry, and secrets hidden in our winding city streets all still resonate and frighten us to this day.

The Terror Beneath Reading List

If you're less familiar with Machen's tales of horror it's recommended you read the following (most, if not all, are available to read free online):

- *The White People*
- *The Great God Pan*
- *The Novel of the Black Seal*
- *The Novel of the White Powder*
- *Ornaments in Jade*
- *The Inmost Light*
- *Out of the Earth*
- *The Lost Club*
- *The Terror*
- *The Shining Pyramid*
- *The Hill of Dreams*
- *The Red Hand*
- *A Fragment of Life*
- *The Green Round*
- *N*

- Contacting an ancient pagan deity in one of its forms (*The Great God Pan*).
- The slow realisation that the world isn't as it seems, with the mundane giving way to the fantastic (*A Fragment of Life*).
- Discovering murderous hidden beings of folklore lurking in the countryside (*The Shining Pyramid*).
- Traversing the Veil between Earth and the Otherworld (*The White People*).
- Scientists mixing technology and occult rites with disastrous consequences (*The Inmost Light*).
- Discovering strange places that exist outside of space and time (*N*).
- Secret societies with bizarre and frightening rituals (*The Lost Club*).
- Ancient beings arriving in industrialised London (*The Red Hand*).
- The corruption of innocents with dark folk magic (*The White People*).

• • •

WHAT IS WEIRD FOLK HORROR?

The taxonomy of horror subgenres is admittedly a bit of a mire. Machen's stories are especially difficult to categorise, with hallmarks of cosmic horror intertwined with the rustic chills of folk horror and the science fiction trappings of weird fiction. *The Terror Beneath* uses the term 'weird folk horror' to describe this particular 'Machenesque' genre, encompassing strange Otherworldliness, pagan terror and science gone awry. Because this game expands on Machen's mythos, for want of a better word, having a term such as weird folk horror makes it easier to understand what sort of stories and monsters fit into this world. A ghost haunting a mansion isn't weird folk horror, but a scientist building a machine to communicate with an ancient horned god is. A weird folk horror mystery will likely have a mix of the following:

A NOTE ON THE REPRESENTATION OF PAGANISM IN THIS GAME

Machen was a dyed-in-the-wool Christian (though with ties to the occult) and so his horror comes from the idea that something predating the Church has survived and is attempting to corrupt the innocent. However, modern-day pagans exist and the notion of paganism as evil is admittedly quite silly. Therefore, while this game tries to stay true to the lurking terrors that Machen described in his stories, it isn't doing so at the expense of real people's beliefs. This is, of course, a fantasy and should be treated as such.

THE TERROR BENEATH'S SETTINGS

While Machen's most prominent works of weird folk horror were written in the waning years of the nineteenth century, the action in *The Terror Beneath* is set in the wake of the Great War. Moving the backdrop from the late Victorian period to the Jazz Age cements some of the themes that are most prominent in Machen's tales: of rapid industrialisation, strange science and a society that is gaining more freedom to express itself. In *The Terror Beneath* these monumental changes brought on by the Great War are the trigger for the Otherworld's assault on Britain.

There are two key setting locations that investigations take place in: the **London Metropolis** and the **Welsh Wilderness**. Throughout a campaign, PCs will explore both settings to uncover the terrible secrets they each hold. Occasionally a mystery will span both settings, perhaps starting to unravel the mystery in a Kensington flat before taking a car to an abandoned farmstead in Pwllheli later in the game.

• • •

THE LONDON METROPOLIS

Investigations in the London Metropolis will see the characters rubbing shoulders with Bright Young Things working pagan magic in Soho, investigating government officials inducted into the Cult of Dionysus, uncovering unexplained slayings in Whitechapel and preventing rogue scientists from the University of London from opening pathways to the Otherworld in the Underground. London is an incredible playground for occult adventure and this book includes ideas and locations you can use to create mysteries of intrigue, mad science and pagan conspiracy.

THE WELSH WILDERNESS

The Welsh Wilderness, on the other hand, leads to investigations that feel like they take place in another time period. Characters will delve into the Black Mountains on the trail of ancient beings, witness witch cult rituals in the Neolithic tomb of Pentre Ifan, uncover the mystery of an abandoned village in Radnor and seek out ancient tablets containing forbidden languages in Glamorgan. You can think of the Welsh Wilderness setting as something more akin to typical folk horror where the countryside itself is the enemy and those who inhabit it have secret knowledge that threaten the lives and sanity of others. This book contains a plethora of cults and eerie locations in which to set your investigations.

THE OTHERWORLD

For millennia humans have known of the existence of a place beyond our own, a domain of strange gods and unearthly beings. In Irish folklore it was called Tír nAill ('the other land'), in Wales it was Annwn, in the legends of King Arthur it was Avalon, and the Green Book identifies it as Deep Dendo. Some tales say the Otherworld is a place of joy and prosperity, a heavenly vista where great stone cities rise from the clouds and the fair folk dance their merry processions. Other stories speak of an underworld where the dead go to their final rest in the care of the horned god Arawn. The truth is much darker than these hearth-told tales would have you believe.

• • •

A TWISTED DOMAIN

Few have passed through the Veil into the domain of the Great Gods and returned with their personality intact. One of the best accounts of a human in the Otherworld is told in the Green Book, detailing a young girl's probing journey into a twisted, seductive landscape where awful creatures conducted strange ceremonies and no stars shone in the night sky. Black forests span endlessly, harbouring nightmarish beings.

Spires, pyramids and standing stones dot the landscape, each playing an unknown part in the bizarre rites conducted by the 'wee folk'. The very landscape is crafted to enchant those who cross into the Otherworld so they might remain there for eternity.

• • •

THE GREAT GODS

The Otherworld is ruled by powerful entities called Great Gods who were once worshipped by our pagan ancestors and whose images adorned shrines, talismans and temples. These gods once took forms pleasant to the human eye, avatars in the shape of humanity that could be sculpted from clay and worshipped by the bonfire. Yet their true forms lurk in the Otherworld as malign, impossible structures that would be horrifying to gaze upon. Each Great God is master over a domain: Pan reigns over the infinite forest, Nodens the terrible ocean, Arawn the chthonic realm below, and more besides. These deities are jealous and megalomaniacal, each attempting to gain even a fragment of the power they used to have in order to hold sway over our own world. Should even one Great God manage to tear through the fabric of reality, civilisation as we know it will meet a horrifying end.

DOORWAYS TO THE OTHERWORLD

Accessing the Otherworld can be as simple as following a cave tunnel or as complex as conducting a sorcerous ritual at a burial mound. Hundreds of folk tales deal with wanderers who hear odd music in the fens only to arrive in the Otherworld after trying to discover its source, or someone receiving a fairy gift that transports them to the land of the fair folk. But for those who want to reach the Otherworld, waiting to randomly stumble on a doorway is out of the question. Scientists hired by the British government have spent decades using a potent mixture of chemistry, alchemy and magical devices to conjure their own routes to the world beyond, usually ending in tragedy for all involved.

SHOULD THE INVESTIGATORS VISIT THE OTHERWORLD?

Being a place that few mortals have entered, the Otherworld shouldn't be a location the PCs just pop over to like they're taking a jaunt to the seaside. Throughout their investigations they should catch small glimpses of the Otherworld: a sketchbook of bizarre animal-featured monoliths, a partially burnt photograph of a starless sky, a vision of a horned figure within a scrying mirror, or a mind-altered government researcher (all with their requisite risks to gain Shock cards). Stepping beyond the Veil should be a crescendo of terror towards the end of the campaign. This should be sold to the players as a truly alien place where the air is curdled with dread.

THE GOLD TIBERIUS SOCIETY

'And I for my part,' said Dyson, 'go forth like a knight-errant in search of adventure. Not that I shall need to seek; rather adventure will seek me; I shall be like a spider in the midst of his web, responsive to every movement, and ever on the alert.'

Adventure of the Gold Tiberius

Each day the people of London go about their business: merchants flogging their market wares, shoeshine boys blacking boots on the street corner, warehouse workers clocking in for the morning shift. But only the enlightened few are able to comprehend the true reality that simmers beneath the surface of the capital, the occult web whose harrowing strands stretch from the slums of Spitalfields all the way to the plush heart of Westminster. These awakened souls have glimpsed the horrors beyond the Veil and have chosen to stand against them. They come together as the Gold Tiberius Society, the last bastion against the ancient terrors that threaten to end civilisation.

As a player you will become a member of the Society, giving your own reason for joining as part of character creation. Sometimes with investigative games it can be difficult for the GM to find an excuse for a group of characters to be brought together to delve into a mystery, so the Gold Tiberius Society provides such a framework.

While the Gold Tiberius Society doesn't exist in Machen's works, the root of it comes from his investigative duo Dyson and Phillipps, the prototypical Mulder and Scully of the late nineteenth century. The Society is an idea of what might have happened if Machen had continued writing a series of Dyson stories that existed in their own continuity, bringing together characters from his other famous stories to do battle against the forces of evil, from the streets of London to the wilds of Wales.

THE FOUNDING

June 1885, Red Lion Square. Two men of leisure sat together admiring a gold coin, its legend reading 'Imp. Tiberius Cæsar Augustus'. One of the men, an admirer and follower of the sciences, Mr Phillipps, recognised the coin as the legendary gold Tiberius – the only one of its kind. The other, Mr Dyson, an occult investigator who had found the coin while fleeing from a group of shadowy thugs, decided at that moment he would solve the mystery of the gold Tiberius and who was after it.

Dyson and Phillipps' investigations would take them down a dark path into the heart of occult London and into the Welsh wilds, meeting those who had come face to face with murderous prehistoric beings, a shape-shifting child born of two realities, medicine that transforms people into primordial ooze, and sinister secret organisations. Soon they would be joined by others who had battled the hidden dread reality: Villiers, whose own investigation had seen him defeat the evil offspring of the god Pan himself; Ambrose, the keeper of the Green Book that details a young girl's corruption into sorcery; and Annie Trevors, who had escaped the Otherworld after being kidnapped by the so-called 'fair folk'. Together they formed the Gold Tiberius Society in October 1906, a collective who would use their skills to investigate the strange forces tearing through the Veil.

MAPPING TERROR

As the Society accumulated cases, Villiers updated what he liked to call the Scarlet Map, which showed in red ink where certain types of occult activity had taken place. After years of study and accumulation of mysteries, the Society discovered that hotspots of activity appearing across the capital appeared to criss-cross. Not only that, strange activity seemed to link directly to events that were occurring in the Welsh countryside, with lines leading directly from known sacred sites in places such as Caerleon to happenings in the heart of the city. Trevors determined these to not be a matter of coincidence, but to have a cause and effect that she called Veins: channels of ancient energy that for whatever reason fed these odd occult occurrences. Trevors believed there could be a wellspring of power from the Otherworld that was spilling into our own and where these Veins intersected was where the Veil between worlds was at its thinnest and could be punctured. This discovery came to be known as the Bleed. Trevors herself would disappear without trace once more in 1916 at the site of a Bleed.

A NEW FRONT

As the machine of war rolled across Europe, the Gold Tiberius Society split their time between helping with the war effort and continuing their occult investigations. After the initial outburst of patriotism in 1914, civilian attitudes towards the war soon soured and as the years drove on the outlook became bleaker. The Society found itself at the mercy of ever darker forces as the devastation of war abroad and at home seemingly corresponded with an influx in Bleed activity. The cases they investigated became increasingly bizarre and cruel, dealing with people utilising the scientific and technological progresses of the war for their own devious ends. Villiers met his own fate during a case where one munitions scientist had devised a new gas using a vile fungus from the Otherworld, turning those who inhaled it into inert zombies. Poor Villiers accidentally took a lung full of the gas and never emerged from the laboratory to which he had tracked the scientist. At this time Phillipps had decided that he would prefer to retire with his body and soul intact, moving away to an estate in Cumbria to spend his days trying to purge his mind of the horrors he had witnessed.

By 1918 and the waning days of the war, Ambrose and Dyson were at loggerheads.

Dyson, still mourning the loss of his friend Villiers, wanted to shutter the Society and all further investigations. He himself now bore the physical and mental scars of their adventures together and had become exhausted by the whole ordeal. Ambrose, on the other hand, believed stopping now could lead to an unfathomable event in the future that could see the Otherworld finally leak into our world, upending civilisation. Dyson would leave to live a hermetic life in the Scottish Borders while Ambrose took it upon himself to continue the legacy of the Society – but he would need help.

THE INVITATION

Ambrose soon set to work gathering like-minded individuals into the fold. Above all else, Ambrose was a man of the streets whose connections across London ran far and wide, from the gutters to the gentry. He sought out those who had seen beyond the Veil; whose reaction to the horrors they witnessed turned to curiosity rather than revulsion. He chose carefully those who had specific skill-sets, posting each of them an invitation letter in a black envelope sealed with golden wax in the shape of the Tiberius. The letter read: 'We have just begun to navigate a strange region; we must expect to encounter strange adventures, strange perils. Report to Mr Ambrose under the sign of the Calthorpe Arms, Holborn, at dusk with the will to uncover what lies beneath our feet.'

Before long Ambrose met with several recipients of the cryptic invitation and, once he had explained who he was and what he wanted of them, he took them to the Society headquarters where he unfurled the Scarlet Map and explained the terrible truth of reality.

THE SOCIETY TODAY

Since its creation the Society has expanded its accommodation in Red Lion Square, Holborn, to take up several flats. Cases crammed with curiosities line the walls and musty piles of yellowing books containing historical and occult writings are stacked throughout the various rooms. Ambrose himself can usually be found stuffed between the pages of a strange tome or scrawling thoughts in his journal. He rarely leaves the confines of the study, due to an old leg wound he picked up in his previous adventures. Instead, he hears rumours from his informants throughout London and scours newspapers looking for strange incidents that could indicate occult activity. Once he discovers an intriguing thread, he briefs the Society to begin their investigation.

CARRYING OUT INVESTIGATIONS FOR THE SOCIETY

In *The Terror Beneath*, players undertake investigations as representatives of the Society, continuing the work Dyson and Phillipps began at the end of the century. It's assumed that investigators have the time and means to spend as long as they wish uncovering the mysteries of the Otherworld and its Veins without being shackled to a day job. Much of this time is spent at Red Lion Square poring over ancient manuscripts, leafing through the forgotten corners of archived newspapers and studying the patterns found in the Scarlet Map. On the occasion where this research doesn't throw up an interesting thread the Society welcomes visitors in need of assistance, having advertised its services by word of mouth throughout London and beyond. While some of these lead to dead ends, others can turn into sprawling adventures leading to a hidden horror that must be extinguished, often by methods strange and occult. The poor souls who seek the Society's aid are often let down by the police, sometimes by ineptitude or laziness and other times because the constabulary fails to explain the unexplainable. On rare occasions, Ambrose has had visits from Scotland Yard pleading for help on a case that has gone beyond their training. In such cases the Society has been able to access valuable police records and autopsy reports, but it's important to stress how uncommon this is.

The study of Veins is an important duty for the Society, continuing Trevors' research into these strange lines of energy that spill out from the Otherworld. As the source of many of these Veins originate in the wilds of Wales it's common for investigators to take trips to that country where the Veil is thinner than anywhere else in Britain. Ambrose usually funds these excursions as investigators stay in hillside bothies, village bed and breakfasts or seaside hotels. There is never a shortage of Welsh newspapers in the Society headquarters to rifle through in search of the fantastic and terrifying.

Where are Trevors and Villiers?

The disappearances of Trevors and Villiers is a mystery that could form the basis of a single investigation or a full campaign. It's not confirmed how Trevors ended up back in the Otherworld, but there was evidence of sorcerous discharge (a mildew-like dusting) at the alleged site of her disappearance in the Black Mountains. You may want to bring Trevors back at a dramatic moment in the campaign, having been altered by her second captivity in the Otherworld. Perhaps she has become corrupted by Pan and seeks the downfall of the Gold Tiberius Society. Or maybe she comes with garbled portents of the future that she has long since lost the ability to articulate.

Villiers could easily be dead or comatose, but those are the least interesting options. Could his inert condition be exploited by a mad scientist looking to create a vessel for an ancient deity? Or maybe he and others like him could act as lighting rods to increase Bleed during a pagan ceremony.

Inviting the Players

The beginning of any *The Terror Beneath* campaign starts with Ambrose's invitation to join the Gold Tiberius Society and become amateur occult investigators. Why each PC received an invitation is covered as part of character creation, but GMs are encouraged to send the players their own physical invitation in a black envelope to really kick-start the campaign in an intriguing way – whether this is handed out to each at the table or dispatched directly to their homes. Just imagine the delight in their eyes when they open their very own invitation to the Gold Tiberius Society.

INVESTIGATOR CREATION

I dream in fire but work in clay.
The Hill of Dreams

In *The Terror Beneath* you take on the roles of members of the Gold Tiberius Society, using the skills obtained by your occupation and background to investigate the Otherworld's incursion into our reality. These investigations are inspired by the horror stories of Arthur Machen, whose narratives saw characters plunge into occult mysteries involving ancient deities such as Pan, hideous monstrous beings in the hills, and hidden societies holding dangerous arcane knowledge. This game builds on Machen's mythology even further by introducing new elements in-keeping with his vision of pagan terror and mad science, and you should feel free to include your own creations in your adventures.

MODES OF PLAY

When creating characters, the group decides which mode they want to play in. Each changes the game's difficulty slightly (though it's never going to be easy):

- **Terror:** This is the least forgiving mode, increasing the lethality of mysteries. Gaining 3 Shock or 3 Injury cards will be the end of a character in this mode. When opting for Terror, you should warn the players in advance that there is a real threat to their characters' safety and as such they should consider their actions more carefully. This is particularly important for players who are new to investigative horror or are used to a more heroic style game.
- **Pulp:** Increases the survivability of characters, if only by a little. Gaining 4 Shock or 4 Injury cards will be enough

to end their careers in this mode. Machen's stories aren't exactly pulpy but if you're wanting to run a game where it's more likely that every investigator will walk out on their own two legs, use Pulp mode. This also works well for a one-shot or convention setting, where death or a broken mind could lead to a player sitting around for an hour twiddling their thumbs.

CREATING YOUR INVESTIGATOR

Each character has come to the Gold Tiberius Society in their own way, with varied backgrounds and occupations. It is assumed that either characters have recently received a windfall and no longer need to work, dedicating their time to the Society, or they still work part time and attend to Society business on the side. The former set-up is more Machenesque, which gives characters ample time to rush off into the wild blue yonder seeking mysteries, but the latter gives a great excuse if a player is missing for a session (their character had urgent business to attend to).

Regardless, all characters are based in the city of London, though they may originate from anywhere in the world. While the 1919 Aliens Restriction Act and subsequent Aliens Order 1920 put heavy restrictions on who could be allowed to work where (such as foreigners being barred from working on British ships), you may decide to agree as a group to ignore these historical rules for ease of play and inclusivity. Sadly, people of colour faced widespread discrimination in the early twentieth century, with race riots exploding in 1919. In a game focused on a specific time period in history, it's important to reflect on the social attitudes of past generations and to understand what you as a player will and won't tolerate in your game. The general rule of thumb is that if everyone at the table is comfortable with including these elements in the game and will treat them respectfully and sensitively, keep your setting historically accurate. However, if even a single player is uncomfortable with this, please ignore these elements. This holds true even if you're halfway through a mystery and a player raises their discomfort.

Each investigator is created by combining two kits: **Occupation Kit** and **Background Kit**.

• • •

OCCUPATION KITS

The Occupation Kit determines the character's investigative skills derived from their job or field of study. Each of these **Investigative abilities** helps them discover clues during an investigation. Investigative abilities written in *italics* represent

Interpersonal abilities. These are abilities that help characters draw clues from people using social skills. Some card effects will ask for an Interpersonal Push, which uses one of the italicised abilities.

Each player decides on a kit to take, noting down their Investigative abilities. Where there are fewer than seven players, the group evenly splits abilities between them from the kits that are remaining, offering reasons as to why their characters would have these skills.

> Seeta, Jerome, Jiro and Elaine are creating their characters, which means the group is down by three players. They take Journalist, Scientist, Museum Curator and Bright Young Thing respectively, splitting the remaining abilities from Pulp Novelist, Antiquarian and Rambler between them.

If there are more than seven players, those without an Occupation Kit may choose four Investigative abilities from any kit to create their own, as long as they don't have duplicates.

Antiquarian

As an antiquarian you can usually be found buried under piles of decaying tomes, strange pottery and ancient artworks in your studies of historical artefacts. Antiquarians are masters of the strange, truffling through the forest of folklore and odd pieces of history lost to time. Modern society scoffs at the humble antiquarian, who is often seen as an eccentric obsessive of unimportant objects, but you would beg to differ. Through each artefact unearthed from the vastness of time you piece together the web of human culture and delve deeply into the secrets of our ancestors. As an investigator you bring your knowledge of the esoteric to the fore, identifying folk objects, songs and legends from a lost age and decoding mysteries lost to time.

Investigative Abilities: Ancient History, Archaeology, Folklore, *Reassurance*.

Bright Young Thing

The Great War was responsible for snuffing the spark of youth, which is why in the 1920s young bohemians in London took life by the hedonistic horns. The tabloids called these partying socialites 'Bright Young Things': flamboyant dressers who threw elaborate parties and drank to excess. This was an optimistic new generation, one born from the horrors of war, who shirked responsibilities to indulge in new pleasures. As a Bright Young Thing, you're not only the soul of the party but you're also well-connected to the fresh heartbeat of London culture. From artists to poets, you rub shoulders with the tastemakers of the day, which makes you a valuable investigator, understanding how to navigate the movers and shakers of this hip new scene.

Investigative Abilities: *Charm,* Culture, *Inspiration, Society.*

Journalist

The journalist is the denizen of Fleet Street, working for top papers such *The Times* and *The Illustrated London News*, getting the scoop through hard investigative graft. Your skills as a journalist come in handy when uncovering occult mysteries: your ability to profile people, your knowledge of the inner workings of London town and your knack for sniffing out a good story. You might be a news hound for one of the big papers, getting to the scene of crimes and disasters as fast as the police (maybe sometimes faster). Or you may be a feature writer for a magazine, crafting persuasive editorials and writing exposes on the rich and powerful.

Investigative Abilities: *Assess Honesty*, Dérive, Essayist, Notice, *Streetwise*.

Museum Curator

London is home to some of the greatest museums in the world: the British Museum, Natural History Museum and the Imperial War Museum are some that still greet hundreds of thousands of visitors to this day. As a curator you're in charge of collections, meticulously researching a subject area and consulting the organisation on obtaining new artefacts. As such, you know a little bit of everything when it comes to history, from royal lineages and famous battles to the gods worshipped by our Neolithic ancestors. The Gold Tiberius Society is the perfect place to put your knowledge to use.

Investigative Abilities: Military History, Natural History, Religion, Research.

Pulp Novelist

News-stands in the 1920s were crammed with cheap magazines sporting strange and salacious covers, from bizarre multi-tentacled aliens wrestling chisel-jawed young men to women wearing nothing but their underwear in a series of compromising positions. As successors to the Victorian penny dreadfuls, the pulps are an entertaining escape from the drudgery of real life. As a pulp novelist you spend much of your time churning out as many stories as you can, quality be damned. Perhaps you aspire to one day be among the great writers of the day, or maybe you're happy penning heart-pounding yarns and looking forward to your weekly payments. Through your writings you have become an expert researcher, understanding how to quickly and efficiently look up specific texts in the library and you often know exactly where to go to get the knowledge you need.

Investigative Abilities: Linguistics, *Negotiation*, Occultism, Research.

Rambler

While the bright lights, vibrant nightlife and work opportunities brought folks from rural areas into the London metropolis, others are keen to get out and experience the beauty and strangeness that nature has to offer. Rambling became a popular pastime for those wanting to escape the London smog and become enveloped in the great British wilderness. As an experienced rambler you know how to survive in the great outdoors, whether it's the ability to track wildlife or knowing what mushrooms you definitely shouldn't be ingesting. Through your travels you've become accustomed to speaking with rural folk, hearing their stories of fairies, boggarts and unimaginable beings who haunt the quiet countryside. As an investigator you take great care in extracting these tales, knowing that in every bit of ancient folklore there's a truth lurking in the background.

Investigative Abilities: Botany, Natural History, *Oral History*, Outdoor Survival.

Scientist

The 1920s was a time of dramatic innovation from the military to the domestic. This is a time when the first television transmitter was tested at the Royal Institute, the first refrigerators became available and rollercoasters were thrilling holidaymakers at the British seaside. Scientists employed by universities and independent organisations raced to be the first to discover a new breakthrough, and sometimes in doing so opened up new doorways for evil to cross into our world. As a scientist you are on an unending quest for knowledge. You want to know how the world ticks and how technology can be used for the advancement of society. As a member of the Gold Tiberius Society, your understanding of the inner workings is crucial for matching wits with the strange pagan science you frequently encounter.

Investigative Abilities: Biology, Chemistry, Geology, Technology.

Crafting your own Occupation Kit

It's easy to use the Investigative abilities listed here to create your own Occupation Kit. So long as there is the right balance of abilities between each PC, feel free to take from several Occupation Kits to create a new character. This usually works best if everyone decides to create a custom Occupation Kit, as it means you're less likely to have duplicate abilities in the group.

• • •

BACKGROUND KITS

Once each player has selected an Occupation Kit they should now choose a Background Kit. These kits provide the character's **General abilities** rather than those designed to unearth information. This may be how well they can drive an automobile, how accurately they can throw a punch or how perceptive they are when things seem awry. A Background Kit represents what the character was in the past, whether an occupation or simply how that individual was raised.

Conscripted Soldier

You set off for adventure but found only pain in the water-logged trenches of the Great War. But you survived on your skill, determination and a hefty amount of luck.

General Abilities:

Athletics	6	Health	3
Composure	6	Mechanics	0
Driving	2	Preparedness	3
Fighting	7	Sense Trouble	1
First Aid	2	Sneaking	2

Farmhand

You grew up in rural Britain, mucking out pigs, tilling the land and respecting mother nature.

General Abilities:

Athletics	6	Health	5
Composure	7	Mechanics	2
Driving	3	Preparedness	1
Fighting	5	Sense Trouble	0
First Aid	3	Sneaking	0

Field Medic

You've seen the worst wounds that war has to offer while serving on the front line.

General Abilities:

Athletics	2	Health	3
Composure	6	Mechanics	0
Driving	2	Preparedness	3
Fighting	5	Sense Trouble	2
First Aid	7	Sneaking	2

Munitions Factory Worker

You spent the war creating crucial armaments for the boys at the front line, putting your life on the line handling hazardous chemicals and machinery.

General Abilities:

Athletics	5	Health	3
Composure	6	Mechanics	6
Driving	0	Preparedness	3
Fighting	5	Sense Trouble	2
First Aid	1	Sneaking	2

Police Officer

You were a member of the constabulary patrolling the streets of London.

General Abilities:

Athletics	4	Health	3
Composure	6	Mechanics	0
Driving	2	Preparedness	4
Fighting	6	Sense Trouble	4
First Aid	1	Sneaking	2

Pugilist

You put your knuckles to good use, winning prize money by beating the hell out of your opponents, whether legally or outside the watchful eye of the law.

General Abilities:

Athletics	8	Health	5
Composure	6	Mechanics	0
Driving	0	Preparedness	2
Fighting	7	Sense Trouble	3
First Aid	1	Sneaking	0

Raised in an Alley

You began in London's steaming gutter, surviving day to day on scraps while avoiding an untimely demise at the sharp end of a knife.

General Abilities:

Athletics	5	Health	4
Composure	5	Mechanics	0
Driving	0	Preparedness	3
Fighting	7	Sense Trouble	4
First Aid	0	Sneaking	4

Shipbuilder

You spent the war in a shipbuilding yard, building everything from tugboats to dreadnoughts.

General Abilities:

Athletics	7	Health	2
Composure	5	Mechanics	6
Driving	2	Preparedness	3
Fighting	5	Sense Trouble	1
First Aid	1	Sneaking	0

Silver Spoon

You're from rich stock, though you may have fallen far from your aristocratic roots.

General Abilities:

Athletics	5	Health	6
Composure	7	Mechanics	0
Driving	4	Preparedness	2
Fighting	5	Sense Trouble	1
First Aid	2	Sneaking	0

Crafting your own Background Kit

Any player is welcome to create their own background, distributing points among each quality as befits that background concept. To do this, allocate 32 points between each of the ten General abilities. Alternatively, they may take a current Background Kit and move some scores around, provided they remain at 32 points. It should be noted that both Composure and Fighting are crucial abilities for staying alive and bringing either below 6 could mean a swifter doom for that character. Then again, if that's how the player wants their character to be then more power to them!

> One player wants their background to be a British spy. They decide to look at the Conscripted Soldier for inspiration. They move 1 point from First Aid to Sneaking and 1 point from Driving to Sense Trouble.

If you're playing in Pulp mode, increase Composure and Fighting in Background Kits by 1 point and add 1 point to the two highest abilities aside from these. When creating your own Backgrounds use 36 points.

CHARACTER GENDER AND NAME

Players should feel free to choose any gender and sexual orientation for their character without fear they will meet resistance when it comes to playing the game. While twentieth-century women were beginning to make headway in being able to work in typically male-dominated workplaces such as factories, and they were embracing a newfound independence in society, the rights of women were still incredibly poor.

If everyone at the table is comfortable staying true to history then the limitations women would face in the 1920s could be explored in a creative and safe way. By default, the game assumes that women are able to become police officers or ship builders without reprisal, even if this bucks the trend historically. After all, we all play to have fun and discrimination is never fun.

• • •

DRIVE

It's now time for each player to create their character's Drive. This is a personal motivation that gives the investigator a reason to act in a certain way in a given situation. A Drive is a defining feature of that character's personality that answers questions such as: What actions do they take in the face of horror? What compels them to follow a mystery in the face of adversity? What brings them back after all seems to be lost?

Help each player to come up with their Drive, canvassing ideas from the rest of the group so that every investigator has a unique motivation. This can be referred to at an opportune point in the game to consider how their character might act. While players may come up with their own Drives, the following is a list that can be used for inspiration:

Adventure

What's life without a bit of peril? You want to grab life by the horns and see the world, not waste away behind some desk for the remainder of your years. You may be a rogue or an adventurer, or simply an office worker who yearns for greater things.

Companionship

You are quick to build a kinship with those around you and will go out of your way to aid your friends. When all is said and done you wish nothing more than to return with your pals to the drawing room for brandy and cigars, but when you're out on an investigation you will follow your compatriots to the end of the earth (and beyond).

Curiosity

You are but a moth to the flame of mystery. Every bone within your body aches to unravel whatever strange scenario you catch wind of. Danger be damned, you're going to get to the bottom of this even if you die trying.

Desperation

You have nothing left to lose. You may have lost your family and friends, through your own fault or otherwise. Now at your lowest ebb you need something to distract you from your own life and maybe a new adventure that will allow you to get yourself back on your feet.

Duty

You are bound by an iron-clad code of honour that puts duty before self-preservation. Whether for the King or someone close to you, your sense of diligence is renowned. Whether this was drilled into you in your military days or in the schoolyard, you will meet the task head on.

Escapism

When you have peered beyond the Veil, how could you possibly go back to your humdrum, grey life. The thought of continuing your dreary mortal existence frightens you even more than the crawling darkness. Through the Gold Tiberius Society you have been offered a way to break the shackles of commonality and do something interesting for once in your life.

Legacy

You want your name to live on in the annals of history, whether to enshrine your family line in glory or just immortalise yourself as a result of your explorations. You want your forebears to look back at what you have done with pride.

Missing Friend

You are on the trail of a friend or family member who disappeared mysteriously. You won't rest until they're found.

Morbid Fascination

You are curious about the realms of death. What life exists beyond the grave? Can we resurrect those who have passed on? You believe the Veil could hold the answer to such questions. Imagine what you could do with that knowledge.

Religion

You believe you have been ordained by God to stem back the tide of evil that threatens the country, believing the devil himself to be at work.

Show-Off

Wherever the attention is, you want to be at its centre. You're an interesting person with a lot to show for it, so why not flaunt it? Delving into occult mysteries offers you the perfect way to boast to others.

Truth-Seeker

For your whole life you have believed in a single constant, but after you saw beyond the Veil your world has been shattered. Now you are driven by the truth. The more you uncover, the more you want to know. Once one mystery is solved, you're still left with questions that need answering. The truth is out there and you're going to find it.

Veil-Touched

Something from beyond the Veil of the Otherworld has affected you physically or mentally. A strange scar or a cryptic recurring dream – and you will get to the bottom of it.

THE TERROR BENEATH

Before becoming occult investigators, each character faced an event that turned their world upside down. This is the event that triggered their invitation to the Gold Tiberius Society, one that exposed them to the perils of the Otherworld for the first time. This event is known as The Terror Beneath and each player should come up with one for their character, to understand what drew them to become investigators. Some examples are as follows:

- A door that opened into a garden that previously didn't exist.
- The silhouette of a horned figure moving through the woods.
- A neighbour slowly becoming a husk.
- A chanting circle of witches in the wilderness.
- Coded military plans to send soldiers into the Otherworld.
- A metallic voice box emitting a strange, guttural language.
- A dead German spy whose features had become mushroom-like.
- A hound of Annwn stalking the moors.
- A stone depicting Roman centurions fighting a huge dhol.
- A mummified voor body that whispers in the night.
- A many-coloured jewel that rapidly aged the owner.
- A machinist crushed by their own automaton.
- Finding a young girl's book of folk magic and witchcraft.

A player's Terror Beneath can create useful mystery hooks for the GM, so it's worth everyone working together to create exciting and mysterious stories that are tantalising enough for that character to seek out more information.

RELATIONSHIPS

To cap off character creation, each player should determine the Relationships their investigator has to others in the group. This aids with group cohesion and helps elevate the drama of an investigation. Go around the table from left to right asking each player about who their character relies on. Then go back around from right to left asking who their character protects. Each relationship should be unique to that character, so there aren't multiple characters relying on just one.

Ask each player to name a character they **rely on** and a character they **protect**, giving short reasons for both.

> Jiro's character Christopher relies on Victor who seems to have a good grasp of the London streets. Christopher also protects Vera, who he sees as physically vulnerable.

CHARACTER CREATION EXAMPLE

Jesse is creating a new character, deciding on the Journalist as their Occupation Kit and Silver Spoon as their Background Kit. They essentially envision a character who's had a privileged upbringing, safe from the horrors of the war. Jesse names the character Sam Chesterton, who uses the pen name S. C. Fife in their writings for *The Times*. As a new journalist, Sam is all about getting to the truth that lies at the heart of every story, so chooses the Drive Truth-Seeker. But how did Sam get drawn into the Gold Tiberius Society? Quite simply through some good old investigative journalism. When following up on a lead around a murder in Knightsbridge, Sam discovered a hidden room covered in strange writings. Worst of all was when he opened a cabinet to find the shrivelled corpse of a voor preserved in formaldehyde labelled 'The Caerleon Specimen'. Finally, Jesse works with the other players on their Relationships, deciding who Sam relies on (a muscle-bound pugilist called Big Ernie) and who Sam protects (a curator called Franny).

INVESTIGATIVE ABILITIES

Mysteries are nothing without a varied range of clues leading the protagonists towards the awful truth at the heart of the investigation. Investigative abilities are your character's way of uncovering clues without the need to roll: if you have the right Investigative ability, you gain the clue.

• • •

INVESTIGATIVE ABILITY DESCRIPTIONS

Ability descriptions consist of a brief general description, followed by examples of their use in an investigation. Creative players should be able to propose additional uses for their abilities as unexpected situations confront their characters. Investigative abilities are divided into the following sub-groups: Academic, Interpersonal, and Technical. The purpose of the sub-groups is to allow you to quickly find the best ability for the task during play, by scanning the most likely portion of the overall list.

Ancient History (Academic)

You are an expert in early human history from around 3000 BCE to roughly 6th century CE. You can:

- Recall the cultural practices of peoples in the time period (such as Celtic tribes).
- Identify symbols, writings and markings used by ancient peoples.
- Understand the hierarchy of ancient tribes and cultures.
- Spot anachronisms or inaccuracies in the research of ancient peoples.

Archaeology (Academic)

Through excavation you delve deep into the ancient world. You're an expert in ancient artefacts, forgotten cultures and things that should perhaps have been left buried. You can:

- Tell how long something has been buried.
- Identify artefacts by culture and usage.
- Distinguish real artefacts from fakes.
- Navigate inside ruins and catacombs.
- Describe the customs of ancient or historical cultures.
- Spot well-disguised graves and underground hiding places.

Assess Honesty (Interpersonal)

You have a knack for telling when someone is hiding the truth from you by reading their facial expressions, body language and tonal intonation. While you get a feeling that someone is lying to you, discerning the lie's motivation is difficult. By spending a Push you may begin to understand such a motivation.

Biology (Academic)

You have knowledge of the workings of the human body, from brain function to muscular structure. You can:

- Identify the symptoms and cause of diseases and infections.
- Know if a person's physiology isn't quite right.
- Give a rough indication of how life-threatening a wound is.
- Know how to lower the risk of harm through rudimentary surgery.

Botany (Academic)

You study plants and fungi and can:

- Identify the likely environment in which a plant sample grew.
- Identify plants which might be toxic, carnivorous, or otherwise dangerous.
- Spot the symptoms of plant-derived poisonings.

Charm (Interpersonal)

You're good at making people want to help you, whether you utilise compliments, flattery or flirting. You can get them to:

- Reveal information.
- Perform minor favours.
- Regard you as trustworthy.
- Become enamoured with you.

Chemistry (Technical)

You're trained in the analysis of chemical substances. You can:

- Among a wide variety of other materials, identify drugs, pharmaceuticals, toxins, and viruses.
- Match samples of dirt or vegetation from a piece of evidence to a scene.

Culture (Academic)

As a general follower of the arts, your knowledge fills in the gaps between other characters' more form-specific awareness of the city's cultural scene. You know the people, trends and venues of such art forms as:

- Dance.
- Music.
- Drama.
- Opera.
- Music hall.
- Ceramics.
- Calligraphy.
- Stage magic.
- Clowning, mime and circus performance.
- Cinema.

Dérive (Academic)

You frequently walk the streets of London with no real motive other than to experience the city. Through your metropolitan journeys you notice elements that passersby don't, whether it's a mysterious park in a secluded part of town, patterns in architecture, or just the general 'feel' of a place. With this you can:

- Recall obscure locations around London.
- Notice architectural detail that has changed over time.
- Know which neighbourhoods are dangerous and which are safe.
- Know shortcuts and hiding places within the city.

Essayist (Academic)

As an essayist you are a well-read member of the literati and a dab hand with the typewriter. You can:

- Identify rich, powerful, and influential persons in your city.
- Recall their past exploits and associations, including those too scandalous to print.
- Name their allies and enemies.
- Understand their political and philosophical leanings.
- Argue in a witty and tendentious style, in person or on the page.
- Navigate the city's profusion of newspapers and journals, from the size of their readership to the quirks of their editors.
- Recall the gist of articles from local publications, no matter how obscure.
- You can also treat this as an Interpersonal ability, prying information from otherwise reluctant witnesses by either promising them favourable coverage, or agreeing not to print what you know about them.

Folklore (Academic)

You have studied the vast folklore of the British Isles and have become knowledgeable about traditions, songs, material culture and local legends. You can:

- Identify the use of a folk item (e.g. a corn doll).
- Know specific dates of the folklore calendar year and what they mean.
- Understand where a certain folk song or dance originated from.
- Bring to mind local legends and myths.

Inspiration (Interpersonal)

You convince reluctant witnesses to supply information by appealing to their better selves. After a few moments of interaction, you intuitively sense the positive values they hold dearest, then invoke them in a brief but stirring speech.

Geology (Academic)

You are an expert on rocks, soils, minerals and the primordial history of the Earth. You can:

- Analyse soil samples, crystals, minerals and so forth.
- Determine the age of a rock stratum.
- Date and identify fossils.
- Evaluate soil for agriculture or industry.
- Identify promising sites for oil or water wells, mines and similar features.

Linguistics (Academic)

You are an expert in the principles and structures underlying languages. You can probably speak other languages, but that is a separate ability that must be purchased separately. You can:

- Given a large enough sample of text, decipher the basic meaning of an unknown language.
- Identify the languages most similar to an unknown language.

- Identify artificial, Otherworldly and constructed languages.

Military History (Academic)

Having studied wars and warfare, you can:

- Inspect weapons, identifying their approximate age, condition, country of origin and manufacturer, specifying whether they were made for civilian or military use.
- Identify battlefields, reconstructing the engagements fought there.
- Recall famous battles and the tactics that determined their victors.
- Tell the rank and specialty of a soldier, past or present, from their uniform.

Natural History (Academic)

You study the evolution, behaviour and biology of plants and animals. You can:

- Tell when an animal is behaving strangely.
- Tell whether an animal or plant is natural to a given area.
- Identify an animal from samples of its hair, blood, bones or other tissue.
- Identify a plant from a small sample.

Negotiation (Interpersonal)

You are an expert in making deals with others, convincing them that the best arrangement for you is also the best for them. You can:

- Haggle for goods and services.
- Mediate hostage situations.
- Swap favours or information with others.

Notice (Technical)

You are adept at noticing subtle details and finding important clues. This is the generic ability for spotting a hidden clue or a disguised imposter, maintaining general situational awareness or noticing a nonthreatening visual anomaly. You can:

- Spot hidden objects and objects of interest at an investigation site.
- Notice subtle errors in a disguise.
- Case a location to spot guards, multiple entrances, potential security response and the like.
- Notice signs of a previous search of the location.
- Note relationships between objects at a crime scene, reconstructing sequences of events.
- Cold read someone, analysing their body language and behaviour to draw conclusions about them.

Occultism (Academic)

You're an expert in the historical study of magic, superstition and hermetic practice from the Stone Age to the present. From the Cult of Dionysus to the Golden Dawn, you know the dates, the places, the controversies and the anecdotes. You can:

- Identify the cultural traditions informing a ritual from examining its physical aftermath.
- Supply historical facts concerning various occult traditions.
- Guess the intended effect of a ritual from its physical aftermath.
- Identify occult activities as the work of informed practitioners or amateurs.

Oral History (Interpersonal)

You can find sources willing to talk, win their confidence and gather (usually lengthy) oral testimony about historical events, local traditions, folklore, family legend or gossip. This is an excellent way to do research in illiterate or semi-literate societies, and in rural or small-town communities in general. This ability also covers taking notes without worrying your sources.

Outdoor Survival (Technical)

You have lived and worked outdoors and in the wild, possibly during a rural upbringing or isolated military service. You can:

- Accurately determine the weather for the next day.
- Tell when an animal is acting strangely.
- Tell whether an animal or plant is natural to a given area and time.
- Hunt, fish and find edible plants.
- Ride a horse (using Athletics to determine how well).
- Make fire and survive outdoors at night or in bad weather.
- Navigate overland.
- Track people, animals or vehicles across grass or through forests.

Reassurance (Interpersonal)

You get people to do what you want by putting them at ease. You can:

- Elicit information and minor favours.
- Allay fear or panic in others.
- Instil a sense of calm during a crisis.

Religion (Academic)

You study religions in their various forms, both ancient and modern. You can:

- Supply information about religious practices and beliefs.
- Quote relevant tags from the major scriptures.
- Recognize the names and attributes of various saints, gods and other figures of religious worship and veneration.
- Identify whether a given religious practice or ritual is orthodox or heretical.
- Fake (or in some traditions, officiate at) a religious ceremony.

Research (Academic)

You know how to find factual information from books, records and official sources. Your contacts pocket book brims with the names and addresses of exotic and useful contacts. On a Push you may gain access to particularly rare tomes or records.

Society (Interpersonal)

Accustomed to travelling in polite society, you understand the etiquette and mores of the ruling class and aristocracy. You gain cooperation and information from persons of good standing by winning their trust, as one who knows how to behave and exercise discretion. You know where these people live and how to gain entrance to their rooms to talk to them without arousing suspicion. Regular study of the society pages keeps you up to date on all of the latest betrothals, marriages, births and business arrangements. On a Push, you can gain non-informational favours from society types.

Streetwise (Interpersonal)

You know how to behave among crooks, street urchins, gangsters and the undesirables of the criminal underworld. You can:

- Deploy criminal etiquette to avoid fights and conflicts.
- Identify unsafe locations and dangerous people.
- Gather underworld rumours.

Technology (Technical)

You have a knack for technology, whether it's knowing the inner workings of common machinery or understanding the burgeoning field of electronics. You can:

- Identify how a piece of technology should be used.
- Take apart and rebuild a piece of machinery or electronics.
- Identify the reason why a piece of technology is faulty.
- Notice how a piece of technology could be unsafe.
- Read plans for a device and understand whether it will work or not.

INVESTIGATIVE ABILITY QUICK REFERENCE

Academic			Interpersonal		Technical
Ancient History	Dérive	Military History	Assess Honesty	Oral History	Chemistry
Archaeology	Essayist	Natural History	Charm	Reassurance	Notice
Biology	Folklore	Occultism	Inspiration	Society	Outdoor Survival
Botany	Geology	Religion	Negotiation	Streetwise	Technology
Culture	Linguistics	Research			

GENERAL ABILITIES

While Investigative abilities automatically succeed so long as you have the right ability for the situation, General abilities are used when failure is as interesting as success. Each General ability has a numerical rating that determines how proficient an investigator is with that ability: the lower the rating the less confident or able they are.

The GM may call for a test to be made against a certain General ability. When this happens, the player may spend points from their ability rating to add to the die roll. The GM sets a Difficulty number for that test based on how tough they think the task is: the lower the number, the easier the test. If the result of the roll plus the points spent is equal to or higher than the Difficulty number, the player has succeeded.

Points are deducted from the General ability's **pool**, which is equal to the rating in that ability. If you have 4 in Fighting, that means your Fighting pool is 4. At points in the game the pool and rating may be different, so bear that in mind. Ability pools refresh at certain intervals, detailed later in these rules.

Violet is attempting to creep into an office unnoticed. The GM asks for a Sneaking test, since it would lead to an interesting outcome whether she succeeded or failed. They set the Difficulty as 4, which is average. Violet decides to use a point of Sneaking from her pool and rolls a die, getting a 3. Adding her point, this is a total of 4, meaning she has succeeded in her attempt to move stealthily. If she had failed, the GM would have concocted an interesting consequence that kept the narrative moving forward despite the failure, such as hearing footsteps coming down the hall, or activating a fight.

GENERAL ABILITY DESCRIPTIONS

There are three types of General abilities:

- **Physical:** covering the investigator's strength and athleticism.
- **Presence:** covering the investigator's emotional and mental fortitude.
- **Focus:** covering an amalgamation of the investigator's concentration and physical dexterity.

These categories are used with Shock and Injury cards. Some cards will affect a certain category, such as giving a penalty to Physical abilities.

Athletics (Physical)

Athletics allows you to perform general acts of physical derring-do, from running to jumping to dodging falling objects. Any physical action not covered by another ability, probably falls under the rubric of Athletics.

You will have to pay a Toll, even when otherwise victorious, to avoid taking a Minor Injury. You can use Athletics points (along with Health and Fighting) to pay Tolls.

Composure (Presence)

Composure measures your ability to keep calm under high levels of stress. By keeping a cool head you can calmly navigate an otherwise terrifying or traumatic scenario.

Test Composure when face to face with a being from beyond the Veil, when witnessing a dark unholy rite or casting a foul spell.

Driving (Physical)

You're a skilled defensive driver, capable of wringing high performance from even the most recalcitrant automobile. You can:

- Evade or conduct pursuit.
- Avoid collisions or minimise damage from collisions.
- Spot tampering with a vehicle.
- Conduct emergency repairs.

Fighting (Physical)

Used when you enter into physical struggle with adversaries, including not only combat but also fleeing and pursuit.

You will have to pay a Toll, even when otherwise victorious, to avoid taking a Minor Injury. You can use Fighting points (along with Health and Athletics) to pay Tolls.

First Aid (Focus)

You can treat emergency injuries or illnesses, such as stemming heavy bleeding, saving someone from choking or performing a resuscitation.

Some Injury cards specify a Difficulty number for First Aid. By making a First Aid test and meeting or beating the Difficulty number, the injured investigator can either discard the card or swap it for a Minor Injury (as detailed on the card).

Health (Physical)

Health measures your ability to sustain injuries, resist infection and survive the effects of toxins.

You will have to pay a Toll, even when otherwise victorious, to avoid taking a Minor Injury. You can use Health points (along with Fighting and Athletics) to pay Tolls.

Mechanics (Focus)

You're good at building, repairing and disabling devices, from ancient traps to motor cars. Given the right components, you can create jury-rigged devices from odd bits of scrap.

Preparedness (Presence)

You expertly anticipate the needs of any job by packing a kit efficiently arranged with necessary gear. Assuming you have immediate access to your kit, you can produce whatever object the team needs to overcome an obstacle. You make a simple test; if you succeed, you have the item you want. You needn't do this in advance of the adventure, but can dig into your kit bag (provided you're able to get to it) as the need arises.

Items of obvious utility to an occult investigation do not require a test. These include but are not limited to: note paper, writing implements, common tools and magnifying glasses.

Other abilities imply the possession of basic gear suitable to their core tasks. Characters with First Aid have their own first aid kits; Outdoor Survivalists come with walking gear and common maps. Preparedness does not intrude into their territory. It covers general-purpose investigative equipment, plus oddball items that suddenly come in handy in the course of the story.

The sorts of items you can produce at a moment's notice depend not on your rating or pool, but on narrative credibility. If the GM determines that your possession of an item would seem ludicrous and/or out of genre, you don't get to roll for it. You simply don't have it. Any item which elicits a laugh from the group when suggested is probably out of bounds.

Sense Trouble (Presence)

Keen perceptions allow you to spot signs of potential danger to yourself and others.

Information gained from this ability might save your skins but doesn't directly advance the central mystery. You might use it to:

- Hear someone sneak up on you.
- See an obscured or hidden figure.
- Smell a gas leak.
- Have a bad feeling about your current situation.

Players never know the Difficulty numbers for Sense Trouble before deciding how many points to spend, even in games where GMs generously inform the players of other Difficulty numbers. Players must blindly choose how much to spend. When more than one player is able to make a Sense Trouble test, the group decides which of them makes the attempt. Only one attempt per source of trouble occurs, conducted by the chosen PC.

Sneaking (Physical)

You're good at placing yourself inside places you have no right to be. You can:

- Pick locks.
- Deactivate or evade security systems.
- Move silently.
- Find suitable places for forced entry, and use them.

GENERAL ABILITY QUICK REFERENCE		
Focus	**Physical**	**Presence**
First Aid	Athletics	Composure
Mechanics	Driving	Preparedness
	Fighting	Sense Trouble
	Health	
	Sneaking	

RULES OF PLAY

He hugged the thought that a great part of what he had invented was in the true sense of the word occult: page after page might have been read aloud to the uninitiated without betraying the inner meaning.

The Hill of Dreams

This section deals with how to play *The Terror Beneath*, from carrying out tests to getting into combat.

• • •

DIE ROLLS

All die rolls in *The Terror Beneath* use a single ordinary (six-sided) die, also known as a d6.

TESTS

Tests are used when there's a chance to fail at an ability. They are used at dramatic moments to increase tension and move the investigation in a new direction. Importantly, tests are only used with General abilities and, unlike Investigative abilities, carry a high chance of failure. Failing test results in negative consequences for the PC attempting the task (and perhaps impacting others too). This could mean slipping and falling while trying to outrun a creature in the dark, or causing even more damage to your automobile's engine instead of fixing it. Conversely, succeeding a test means the PC gets what they want out of the action. Their dodgy engine rumbles to life or they manage to duck behind a tree to avoid pursuit.

In a game of pulse-pounding terror, rolling for tests at every opportunity can detract from the mood. Most of the time the GM will allow an automatic success, with possible bonuses when points are spent.

ASSIGNING A DIFFICULTY NUMBER

The GM will secretly assign a **Difficulty number** to a test depending on how simple or tough they want to make the task. Difficulty ranges from 2 (very easy) to 8 (or higher, which is nearly impossible). A Difficulty of 4 is average. While the GM should never tell the player what the number is, they can offer a narrative indication of how tricky the test might be. This can be achieved by saying something like 'Usually you could do this with your eyes closed, but be careful!', 'When you last attempted this you nearly fell flat on your face', or 'You have very little experience in this area so it's a risky undertaking.'

• • •

MAKING THE TEST

The GM will usually tell the player what General ability they need to roll for a test and decide on a Difficulty number. The player then rolls a die. If the result is equal to or above the Difficulty, they succeed. The player can spend any number of points from the relevant ability pool before rolling to gain a bonus to the result based on the points spent in this way. Spent points are deducted from the relevant General ability and only return when they are refreshed.

Annie is frantically trying to escape a cave whose walls and ceiling are rapidly crumbling. To make it out unscathed, the GM calls for an Athletics test, secretly setting the Difficulty number at 6 (a pretty tough test!). With 6 points in Athletics and desperate not to get squashed by a falling boulder, Annie's player spends 4˙ points from her Athletics pool before rolling. She rolls a 5, adding her 4 Athletics points for a total of 9. The GM excitedly narrates how Annie summons up some unearthly strength to sprint out of the cave before the entire structure collapses.

FAILING FORWARDS

Having a failed test put a stop to the game's flow can be frustrating. For instance, if you're trying to break into an office and both the lockpicking and door barging tests fail. This is where failing forwards comes into play. Whenever it makes sense to do so, a failed test should do one of two things:

- Open up a new avenue for the players to succeed; or
- Allow them to succeed a task but with a complication.

In the first instance, if the investigators fail to break into a locked office door, the GM might present them with a new avenue: they remember the security guard had a key on his

belt. In this way they gain a new challenge they may be able to approach in different ways. In the second instance, the GM may decide they do barge the door open, but in doing so take a Toll on their Health from a minor scrape, or make so much noise that they alert a guard down the hall. Here they get what they want but they have either paid a price or ratcheted up the tension.

WHEN YOUR POOL IS 0

Even if an ability pool is at 0 points, you can still make a test as usual. In this case, the roll is unmodified as there are no points to spend.

WHEN YOUR ABILITY RATING IS 0

You can always test any ability, even when you didn't acquire any points in it during character generation. When it breaks story credibility for you to show even rudimentary competence in an ability, your GM may ask you to justify how you could do whatever it is you are doing. When in doubt, suggest that a PC who does have the ability gave you pointers, either directly or through observation.

PIGGYBACKING

When you have a group of investigators acting together, designate one to take the lead. That character makes a simple test, spending any number of their own pool points toward the task, as usual. All other characters pay 1 point from their relevant pools in order to gain the benefits of the leader's action. These points are not added to the leader's die result. For every character who is unable to pay this piggybacking cost, either because they lack pool points or do not have the ability at all, the Difficulty number of the attempt increases by 2.

> The investigators are all too aware of the things that crawl in the dark woods so wish to move quietly. Elaine's character Vera has a Sneaking rating of 2, so she is nominated as leader. Elaine pays 1 point, while Jerome, Seeta and Bob also pay a point. However, Jiro's character has no points left in Sneaking so can't pay, meaning the GM increases the Difficulty from 4 to 6. Elaine rolls a 4 on the die and adds her 2 points, netting her the 6 needed to succeed.

In most instances a group cannot logically act simultaneously. Only one character can drive a car at one time. Two characters with Preparedness check their individual kits in sequence, with the highest spend going first (in the event of a tie, the players may decide), rather than checking a single kit at the same time.

MARGINS

In some special tests or contests, the difference between Difficulty and result is used to determine the degree of failure or success. This number is called the **margin**.

COOPERATION

When two characters cooperate toward a single goal, they agree which of them is undertaking the task directly, and which is assisting. The leader may spend any number of points from a relevant pool, adding them to the die roll. The assistant may pay any number of points from their pool (even a different one, so long as it's relevant). All but one of these points is applied to the die roll.

Christopher and Vera are tearing along a country lane in their car as a pack of spectral hounds chase them down. The GM determines that a Driving test will be needed to lose the hounds, setting the Difficulty at 5. As the driver, Christopher is the lead and spends 3 points of Driving. Vera can't take the wheel but can help by pointing out hazards on the road using Sense Trouble. Her player spends 3 points from Sense Trouble, with only 2 counting towards the total. Christopher's player rolls a 2, adding his 3 Driving points and Vera's 2 Sense Trouble points for a total of 7 – a success!

SPENDS

There will be occasions when a character is going to succeed at a task, even if there's a slight amount of challenge involved. In this instance, don't worry about having them take a Toll for the task. Instead, charge them a number of points from relevant General ability pools, called a **spend**. Spends can be paid by one character, or multiple players might chip in.

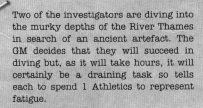

Two of the investigators are diving into the murky depths of the River Thames in search of an ancient artefact. The GM decides that they will succeed in diving but, as it will take hours, it will certainly be a draining task so tells each to spend 1 Athletics to represent fatigue.

COMPETITIVE TESTS

Very occasionally PCs compete to see who best performs a task. Each makes a test; the character with the highest result wins. If the result is a tie, the character with the higher spend, then the higher rating, wins. If all of those factors come out even, the characters tie, no matter how odd that might be. In a case where it is possible for everyone to fail, competitors must also beat a Difficulty set by the GM.

Annie challenges Christopher to a friendly game of darts to pass the time. Unless nobody hits the dartboard at all it's almost impossible to fail, so the GM doesn't set a Difficulty. They rule that Composure is more applicable than Athletics here, so Annie spends 2 points from her Composure pool and Christopher spends 3. Annie rolls a 4 for a total of 6, while Christopher rolls a 2 for a total of 5. Annie outscores her fellow investigator on the dartboard and feels pretty smug about the whole thing.

SALIENCE

All tests should advance the narrative in some way and be relevant to whatever is happening in the mystery at that point. In some cases, Injury and Shock cards may allow PCs to gain benefits or discards on a successful test or if a certain condition is met. The GM should only grant these benefits if they make sense to the story, rather than a player attempting to trigger them gratuitously.

The Injury card Something in Your Eye can be discarded after failing a Focus, Physical or Sense Trouble test. But this should only be given where it makes narrative sense. The PC shouldn't be able to discard the Injury for attempting a random Physical roll immediately after receiving the card.

PUSHES

A Push represents a sudden spark of inspiration gained by an investigator while using an Investigative ability. It allows for more benefits than they would get by just using an Investigative ability. However, Pushes should never have to be spent to get information in the first place. Instead, a Push may allow them to gain extra information from an informant, obtain a better-quality item or offer new insight they wouldn't have received by simply using their ability. Pushes are never used on General abilities.

- For example, you could spend an Archaeology Push to:
- Acquire an artefact for a bargain price.

- Establish a friendly prior relationship with a famous archaeologist appearing in the current mystery.
- Expose a sham curator for their lack of knowledge.
- Impress a celebrated historian so much they become friendly towards you.

Some Shock and Injury cards can be discarded by spending a Push.

On occasion the GM may allow players to gain benefits not connected to any ability in the game, in exchange for a Push. For example, a player might ask if a flammable haystack happens to be situated conveniently close to a farmhouse she wants to burn down. That isn't under the character's control in any way, but for the cost of a Push can be put within the player's control.

TIME INCREMENTS

INTERVALS

A new interval begins each time the group acquires a new core clue. When more than one core clue can be gained during a single scene, only the first clue counts as starting a new interval. When a rule says, for example, that something happens after two intervals pass, it means that the group must gather two core clues in separate scenes.

• • •

SESSIONS

A session is the time spent playing one sitting of the game, whatever that happens to be. If your sessions wildly differ from a baseline of three to four hours, you may find yourself adjusting the timing of effects keyed to sessions.

MYSTERIES

An effect that lasts until the end of a mystery concludes when the main answer to a mystery occurs, plus perhaps a brief coda in which the team ties up loose ends, breaks terrible news to grieving relatives, make patrons aware of debts incurred or discharged and so on. Depending on how quickly the players crack the case at hand, a mystery might encompass multiple sessions, or last for one session only.

• • •

WORLD TIME

An hour quite simply means an hour's worth of time. An hour of world time refers to time as it unfolds for the characters. As in a piece of fiction, world time almost never elapses at the same rate for the characters as for the players and GM. A day might pass in a single sentence from the GM: 'A day later, you find yourself at the mountain.' Or you could spend minutes describing an action that in world time takes only a second or two.

GAME TIME

An hour of game time refers to the real-world time you, the GM and players, spend at the gaming table. The distinction between world and game time mostly matters when measuring the duration of Shock and Injury cards.

REFRESHING POINTS AND PUSHES

When points or Pushes return to their starting values, it's called a **refresh**. Pushes refresh to 2 per player at the start of each session. General ability pools return to the value of their ratings at the start of each mystery. This assumes a mystery takes one or two sessions to complete.

GMs may wish to build moments into longer mysteries, or ones in which significant leaps of time occur, which allow General ability points to refresh. When a rule, card text, or mystery refers simply to a refresh, read that to mean a full refresh – the character's pool returns to its full value.

• • •

PARTIAL REFRESHES

In some cases, partial refreshes occur in which the character regains a set number of points.

These are marked with the number of points regained: so in a 2-point refresh, characters can top up their pools by 2 points. Partial refreshes never allow characters to increase their pools above their ratings.

WHEW

One type of partial refresh is the **whew**. It emulates the moment of relief in a narrative when the trepidation surrounding a daunting circumstance turns out to be nothing. Whew! A whew provides a 2-point refresh.

The whew most often applies to Composure. Award one when players clearly dread an upcoming story turn which instead proves completely innocuous:

- A foul gurgling can be heard in the cellar of The Royal Oak pub. With rumours of a strange pale man sighted down there, the investigators cautiously make their way down as the gurgling gets louder and more horrific. Never mind, it's just a sink with dodgy plumbing!
- In the middle of the night, something begins smashing the barn door with the characters inside. They hear the ominous growl of a hound, but when the door splinters open it's just the local farmer and his overly-excited dog. Whew! To maintain the emotional power of the whew, use it sparingly and only when it fits. Often the players will set up a whew for you, by showing genuine terror of an upcoming moment you never intended to play as anything other than innocuous.

Look particularly for situations where the group sends in only some of its members to confront the imagined awfulness. That way, the brave are rewarded and the cautious lose out. Whews that refresh other General abilities don't come easily to mind but if one that makes sense presents itself during play, rule it in.

VEIL BLEED

Bleed is the term for how far the Veil is thinned in an area. Bleed occurs where energy from the Otherworld is passing through into our world, leaving an invisible trace that can warp that location. The strength of Bleed in a location can affect the power of beings as well as unlocking certain sorcerous abilities. In a mystery, some locations will be assigned a Bleed value from 1 to 3 to show how much sway the forces of the Otherworld have here. Mundane locations are considered to be Bleed 0. Beings may use items or abilities to increase Bleed in order to summon forth entities from the Otherworld, such as Great Gods, or to increase the Bleed in a given area.

While Bleed is technically invisible to the human eye, an area of Bleed does inflict unusual sensations and emotions on those who hang around. Don't tell the players what the Bleed level is, but explain how it's physically interacting with them using the guidelines below.

1 Bleed:

- Some light energy crossing from the Otherworld, likely on a sacred line.
- Creatures can't normally cross from the Otherworld.
- Characters feel hairs prickling up on the backs on their necks.

2 Bleed:

- The Veil is thin and ancient beings can cross between worlds momentarily.
- Colours become more vivid and there's a feel of static in the air.

3 Bleed:

- The Veil is at its weakest, with vast amounts of energy spilling out.
- Otherworldly beings and Great Gods may pass through unhindered.
- Colours are saturated and white flowing energy can be physically seen in the periphery.

FIGHTING

Though characters spend most of their time solving mysteries, sometimes the answers they seek lead them into violent conflict. Fight scenes in *The Terror Beneath* unfold in the following stages.

DEFINE OBJECTIVES

- Define the objective of each side.
- The GM chooses for the opposition.
- Players confer to choose their collective objective. If they fail to agree, and any player chooses Kill, that's the objective.

Common objectives are:

- **Kill:** Enter into a bloody conflict that ends only when one side is dead.
- **Render Helpless:** Continue fighting until one side is too hurt to carry on. Helpless opponents remain on the scene. You may take them prisoner or depart as they roll around on the ground in pain. Killing helpless people or intelligent creatures generally requires Composure tests (baseline Difficulty of 6) to avoid Shock. Minor: A Crossed Line; Major: Out of Control.
- **Gain Surrender:** Keep fighting until everyone on the other side agrees to be taken into custody, in exchange for a promise of fair treatment. Not all combatants will willingly surrender. When they don't, the GM treats the situation as if the players have chosen the Render Helpless objective.
- **Beat Up:** Thrash your opponents and walk away, leaving them badly hurt but not dead.
- **Block:** Stop your opponents from moving past you.
- **Drive Away:** Keep fighting until everyone on the other side retreats. If they were attacking you, they flee back to wherever they came from. If they were defending a position, they flee in random directions or back toward the nearest position of safety. Use when you want to defeat your enemy without killing or capturing them.
- **Escape:** Flee to a position of safety the enemy is not attempting to hold or protect.
- **Escape with a Captive:** Grab a member of the opposing force, then flee with your new captive to a position of safety the enemy is not attempting to hold or protect. Where the enemy group includes combatants of varied ability, you take its weakest or most vulnerable member.
- **Gain an Item:** Grab a portable, easily seized item held by a member of the opposing force, then flee with it to a position of safety the enemy is not attempting to hold or protect. Suitable items include books, weapons, amulets, purses, satchels and documents.
- **Overrun:** You forcibly move through a group of opponents attempting to block you from going somewhere.
- **Topple:** You knock the target off its feet – which is only worth doing when your enemy stands on a cliffside, on the brink of a raging river, in a precarious rowboat or in some similar situation where a fall will cause a more-than-momentary setback.

The investigators have entered an illegal laboratory overseen by Professor Whitman, a brain surgeon who has created three husks (bodies who have become the vessels of ancient entities). Their visages hideously twisted, the husks descend on the investigators. The players all agree that they need to subdue these creatures as they are still human beings and the operation that made them into these vile beings could be reversed. Understanding that the husks are unlikely to surrender (having previously fought one off), they opt for the Render Helpless objective.

DETERMINE DIFFICULTY

The GM (or mystery) defines a Difficulty reflecting the overall strength of the entire opposition, including any tactical advantages or disadvantages they may have in this particular situation. Foes described in this book come with assigned Difficulties, but you can always bounce them up and down to fit the logic of your story. Describe situational modifiers to make shifts feel consistent to players.

OPT-OUT PENALTIES

The difficulties outlined in the Relative Challenge Table below suppose that the foe is fighting all PCs. There will be times when another character will be absent or unable to take part in the combat. When this is the case, each PC in the fight suffers a -1 penalty to Fighting for each absent PC. The Toll for any foe in combat also increases by 1. This means that it's a much better idea for investigators to stick together, but provides an interesting conundrum where they want to be efficient and be in two places at once.

RELATIVE CHALLENGE TABLE				
Relative Challenge	Difficulty (Escape)	Difficulty (Other)	Difficulty (Kill)	Toll
Weak	2	2	3	0
Tough but Outmatched	2	2	4	0
Evenly Matched	3	4	5	1
Superior	3	4	6	1
Vastly Superior	3	6	7	2
Overwhelming	4	7	8	3
Too Awful to Contemplate	5	8	10	4

TOLLS

The other key game statistic for a foe, listed above, is its **Toll**.

Even a protagonist who wins a fight sometimes gets bashed up along the way. Tolls represent the negligible bumps, scrapes, jars and jolts investigators sustain as they dish out worse to their enemies.

Players pay Tolls from any combination of Athletics, Fighting and Health. Characters who can't or won't pay the Toll instead take foe's Minor Injury card.

As you can see from the above table, only the more formidable foes, who will knock you around a bit before you put them down, impose Tolls.

In standard GUMSHOE, the equivalent of a Toll is a Health point loss that leaves you above 0 Health. You might also compare them to the small hit point losses common to other roleplaying games.

• • •

FIGHT TRACKER

To aid you in running the fight, ready a copy of the Fight Tracker (a blank version is shown below).

Player					
Spend					
Margin					
Total					

Write the names of the players attending the current session in the row marked 'Player'. You probably want to use their seating order from left to right but any order will do.

Player	Jiro	Seeta	Elaine	Bob	Jerome
Spend					
Margin					
Total					

Declare Spends

Ask each player in turn how many Fighting points they're spending on the coming test. Enter this number in the 'Spend' row.

> Jiro, Seeta and Bob all say they're spending 3 points. Jerome tells you he's spending 4. Elaine only has 1 to spend.

Player	Jiro	Seeta	Elaine	Bob	Jerome
Spend	3	3	1	3	4
Margin					
Total					

Determine Order of Action

Players are about to take turns, in the following order:

1. High spends go first. Players spending 0 points go last.
2. When two or more players are making the same spend, the ones seated on the left (from your point of view) go before those seated on the right.

> Jerome is spending more than anyone, at 4 points. He goes first. Then come the players spending 3, from left to right: Jiro, Seeta and Bob. Finally, comes, Elaine, spending 1.

In an online game without an apparent seating order, break ties in the order of action in whatever manner you find most intuitive. Alphabetical by player or character name probably works best. Does the platform you're using create a virtual seating order? Use that.

Alternate Rule

Some groups prefer to reverse the order of action, going from lowest to highest spends. This choice values narrative clarity over suspense. It allows players of the characters delivering what are likely to be the finishing blows to describe the definitive actions they take to beat the foe. If they win, that is.

Players Take Their Turns

Players take individual turns, in which they:

1. Describe what they're hoping to physically accomplish in the fight.
2. Make Fighting tests.
3. Compare Fighting test results against the foe's Difficulty number, including applicable modifiers.
   a. Players who meet or beat the number:
      i. Describe themselves successfully doing what they set out to do in step 1.
      ii. Must either pay the foe's Toll (if any) or take its Minor Injury card. (A few foes instead deal out Shocks.) The Toll, listed in the foe's profile, can be paid from any combination of Fighting, Athletics or Health. If they take the Injury, you narrate how they suffer it, based on the card's title and text.
   B. If they do not meet or beat the number:
      i. You describe their chosen opponent defeating their attempt.
      ii. On a margin of 0 or 1, they take the foe's Minor Injury card.
      iii. On a higher margin, they take the foe's Major Injury card.
4. You mark the player's margin, which may be positive, negative or zero, under their column in the margin row of the fight tracker. If the margin exceeds 3, it truncates, becoming a 3. Players whose margins are truncated get a Fight Benefit at the end of the fight, so mark this by underlining any truncated margin.
5. If other players have already acted, add the player's margin to the running combined total of all previous margins. Cross out the margin for the last player who acted. Call out the new running margin to the players.
   a. If it is positive or zero, describe how they are collectively triumphing over their adversaries. Zero indicates that they're winning by a hair's breadth.
   B. If it is negative, describe their enemies taking the upper hand in the fight.
   C. As necessary, throw in bits of narration to keep the sense of threat alive
6. If other players have yet to take their turn, return to step 1 with the next player in the order of action.
7. If this player was the last in the turn order, move to the next stage, 'Name the Victors', below.

> Jerome acts first. 'Victor is going to bullrush the closest husk into the wall, attempting to knock it out.' He spent 4 points and rolls a 2, with an outcome of 6. The husk's Difficulty is 4, which means the action succeeds with a margin of 2. However, the husk has a Toll of 1, which Jerome deducts from his Athletics pool. You narrate the scene: 'You manage to grasp the husk around the waist as you run him at full force into the brick wall, but the creature's head recoils into yours giving you a whopping bruise, dazing you for a moment.' You mark down the positive margin of 2 in the Fight Tracker.

Player	Jiro	Seeta	Elaine	Bob	Jerome
Spend	3	3	1	3	4
Margin					2
Total					2

Next comes Jiro, spotting a human-sized chamber the professor was keeping his subject in. 'Christopher will shove the husk closest to the chamber inside and throw the door closed.' He rolls a 5, which added to his 3 points spent gives him an outcome of 8. The margin is truncated to a 3, but you underline the number to show they will gain a Fight Benefit at the end. 'The husk stumbles backwards into the chamber and accidentally knocks a panel as he does, sealing him in. He pounds on the glass with rage, but can't seem to break through.' However, Jiro must take 1 Toll, choosing Health, deciding that the shove took a lot out of Christopher.

Player	Jiro	Seeta	Elaine	Bob	Jerome
Spend	3	3	1	3	4
Margin	3				2
Total	5				2

Emboldened by Jiro's success, Seeta steps up: 'Annie just flat-out lamps one of the husks in the jaw to try to knock it out cold. Her biceps are bulging!' She rolls a 1, which gives her an outcome of 4, meeting the Difficulty and giving a margin of 0. Annie manages to succeed with her punch, but barely. 'You give the creature a good crack, slowing it somewhat but I'm afraid it's not down for the count yet.' Seeta takes a Toll of 1 on Athletics, rationalising that Annie's poor form had hurt her hand.

Player	Jiro	Seeta	Elaine	Bob	Jerome
Spend	3	3	1	3	4
Margin	3	0			2
Total	5	5			2

You tell the group the conflict is going in their favour, having so far racked up a running margin of 5. Bob asks if there is anything lying around that could bind their hands. You decide there's likely to be tubing that can be ripped out of the strange machines that line the walls. 'I'm going to run over and tear out a tube in the hope of tying one of these husk's hands together.' He rolls a 3, adding to his spend of 3 is a success with a margin of 2. You narrate Bob's ingenious manoeuvre as he binds the semi-dazed husk. He takes a Toll of 1 from his Athletics from the struggle.

Player	Jiro	Seeta	Elaine	Bob	Jerome
Spend	3	3	1	3	4
Margin	3	0		2	2
Total	5	5		7	2

With the new group margin at 7, the players are sure to succeed. It's now Elaine's turn, who invested a single point at the beginning of the fight. You remind the group that one husk is still on the loose, though fairly worse for wear after being forced into a wall. Elaine declares, 'Vera will try to pin the beast with a table while it's slumped against the wall.' She rolls a 1, making a personal margin of -2. This means her character will take a Major Injury Card, which for the husk is Badly Beaten. You narrate how the husk springs up with superhuman-like speed, launching itself directly at Vera, knocking her back into the tables. Elaine takes the Toll of 1 from her Health and receives the card.

Player	Jiro	Seeta	Elaine	Bob	Jerome
Spend	3	3	1	3	4
Margin	3	0	-2	2	2
Total	5	5	5	7	2

Name the Victors

When the last player has acted, their entry in the 'Total' row becomes the final group margin.

If it meets or beats 0, the group scores a victory and achieves its declared goal. Invite players with margins higher than 0 to describe the actions they perform to definitively achieve it. Go from highest to lowest margin, breaking ties from low to high spend, then seating order. Did everyone get a 0? Then everyone narrates.

> Jiro, Bob and Jerome all achieved a higher-than-zero margin, so you invite them to narrate. Jiro goes first, as he has the highest margin, while Jerome has the same margin as Bob but a higher spend so Bob goes last.
>
> 'I wrestle the husk from Vera and force it into one of the open chambers, locking it closed,' Jiro says.
>
> 'I begin running to the door to try to catch up with Whitman,' narrates Jerome.
>
> 'I find some extra tubing to bind the husk's legs, making sure it's tight enough that it won't wriggle free,' says Bob.

If not, the GM describes how the opposition thwarts them as they suffer a defeat. Their enemies can't hurt them any further, but they can put them in an otherwise worse situation. Of course, the character who took a third Injury card has been killed by that last Injury.

Characters scoring a margin greater than 3 get a Fight Benefit. They may either:

- Gain a Push; or
- Refresh a General ability other than Fighting, Health or Athletics.

> Checking the Fight Tracker, you note that Jiro's margin is underlined, so he gains a Fight Benefit. He selects to refresh First Aid so he might be able to help Elaine's character with her Major Injury.

Fighting Quick Reference

1. Players define objectives.
2. GM determines Difficulty.
3. GM prepares the Fight Tracker.
4. Players declare spends.
5. GM determines order of action.
6. Participating characters take -1 Fighting and +1 to Tolls for each non-participating character (see p. 53 for exceptions).
7. Next player in order:
   A. Describes what the character is trying to do.
   B. Makes a Fighting test.
   C. On a success, the player:
      i. Narrates a successful action.
      ii. Either:
         a. Pays the foes' Toll; or
         b. Takes a Minor Injury, which the GM narrates.
   D. On a failure:
      i. The GM narrates the foe's successful action.
      ii. On a margin of 0 or 1: the character takes a Minor Injury, which the GM narrates.
      iii. On a higher margin, the character takes a Major Injury, which the GM narrates.
   E. The GM notes the player's margin, truncating margins of 4 or more to 3, and underlining them.
   F. The GM incorporates the player's margin into the group's running total and announces it.
      i. If it is greater than 0, the players narrate a situation in which they have the upper hand.
      ii. Otherwise, the GM narrates a situation in which the foes have the upper hand.
8. When all players have acted, consult the final margin.
   A. If more than 0:
      i. Players whose characters scored margins of 0 or more describe the group achieving its chosen objective.
      ii. Players whose margins were truncated choose to:
         a. a. Gain a Push; or
         b. b. Refresh a General ability other than Fighting, Health or Athletics.
   B. B. If less than 0, the GM describes their failure to achieve the objective, possibly including the circumstances preventing the victorious foe from killing the surviving PCs.

FIGHTING AS A QUICK TEST

There will be times when there's little point in setting up a full combat, instead achieving an objective with succeeding a Fighting test. Treat this as you would any General test. A Quick Fighting test could be used for any of the following:

- Knocking unconscious or restraining a helpless individual.
- Taking a weapon from someone intent on self-harm.
- Hunting a game animal.

If the opponent is actively trying to harm the players, a full combat should be played through.

FIGHTING AT LESS THAN FULL STRENGTH

The Relative Challenge of foes is calculated assuming that they're taking on a full group of PCs. Weaker members of a group may be tempted to sit out a battle and let those with higher Fighting pools take all the risk. This is not a smart move: it gives the enemy a numbers advantage. Even a single foe capable of taking on many heroes will have an easier time against three investigators than it would against four, and easier still against only two adversaries. This is how fights work in any roleplaying game: a dragon has an easier time against a fighter and a cleric than she would against a fighter, a cleric, a wizard and a rogue.

When PCs elect to skip a fight, those who do take part in the battle receive a -1 Fighting penalty per absent comrade. The foe's Toll increases by 1 for each absent PC. This reflects the added challenge and costs of fighting while short-handed.

GMs may choose to ignore the penalty for fighting at less than full strength when it seems punitive or contrary to story logic. Apt times to waive the penalty include:

- When the party is at less than full strength due to circumstances contrived by the GM. If the group splits up and half of them get in a tussle with drunken rival students, or attacked by voor, describe only enough adversaries to threaten half the group, and ignore the penalty. (In group versus group melees, the number of foes you describe is a matter of atmosphere and description.

It can be higher or greater than the size of the PC group without impacting the game mechanics.)
- When players (as opposed to their characters) are absent.
- When a character is not just unwilling but unable to fight due to the effects of a completely debilitating Shock or Injury card.

The GM need never waive the penalty when players bend the story out of shape to justify fighting at less than full strength.

When you waive the penalty, and another fight against the same enemy occurs later, you may need to describe countervailing changes in the situation to explain why they seem just as effective against a larger force of PCs. More likely, however, with die results and spends adding variance to the outcome, no one will notice or care.

SHOCKS AND INJURIES

When a PC is physically or mentally harmed, they gain **Injury** and **Shock** cards representing damage to their body and mind (found at the end of this book). The GM can scan these and print them out if playing around a physical table, or use them as tokens in a virtual tabletop.

Whenever you gain an Injury or Shock card, you add it to your 'hand'. All players should lay their cards out in front of them for all to see. When you have to get rid of a card from your hand it's discarded back into the card pile. If you have a Major Injury or Shock, which represents a particularly dire infliction, you may have to trade it for another card, usually a more tolerable version.

Specific card text overrides general rules, even if it contradicts those rules.

At the end of each mystery, discard all cards that don't contain the text 'Continuity'. Any card without this tag, and without an explicit discard condition, is discarded at the end of a mystery.

The majority of cards have a way of discarding them during the session. This could be succeeding a certain test, paying a Push or doing something narratively. It's up to the GM and players to explain how this is done in the story. If it's something that could happen in your favourite horror novel or film, it's probably worth going with.

When an Injury card lists a First Aid Difficulty, another character with that ability can get rid of the card for you by successfully making that test.

Some cards allow you to fulfil conditions, such as spending General ability points or Pushes, to discard the card. In certain cases, you can do this only after a specified time has elapsed. Where no time is specified, you can get rid of the card immediately, suffering no ill effect other than the expenditure.

• • •

DEATH AND INCAPACITY

A character dies and leaves play for good after receiving too many Injury cards. A character suffers irreparable mental strain and leaves play (played by the GM if the character appears again at all) after receiving too many Shock cards.

- In Terror mode, too many of either Shock or Injury cards = 3. The third Shock or Injury card is called your **Final card**.
- In Pulp mode, too many of either Shock or Injury cards = 4. The fourth Shock or Injury card in either category you take is called your **Final card**.

For example, in Terror mode an investigator could have 2 Injury cards and 2 Shock cards and still be OK (so to speak) but receiving a third Injury would be their Final card.

As soon as you have a third Injury card in your hand, the GM invites you to describe a suitable death, given the circumstances that led to your gaining that fatal third card. You might:

- Take inspiration from the situation currently being narrated.
- Describe an even worse version of the harm implied by the title and effects of the Final card.
- Describe a fatal worsening of a condition suggested by a previous Injury card already in hand.
- Likewise, as soon as you have 3 Shock cards in hand, your character loses all grip on reality. You might:
- Take inspiration from the situation currently being narrated.

- Describe an even worse version of the emotional or perceptual break implied by the title and effects of the Final card.
- Describe a condition suggested by a previous Shock card already in hand shattering the character's psyche.

This could be followed up with a suggestion of the character's eventual fate: commitment to a sanatorium, becoming a shut-in, kept in the family attic, loping off into the woods to live as a hermit or the like. Depending on where the characters are when you take the Final card, you might describe this right away, or after an appropriate break in the action.

After the narration ensuing from a Final card, the player creates a new character, using the guidelines on p. 59.

If you hear a player conclude that their characters only have 3 (or 4) hit points, they're setting themselves up for confusion and annoyance, as that's not how these rules think.

CARD TERMS

As a shorthand, certain cards use standard terms defined here.

+x to Tolls

The character holding the card treats foes as if their Tolls are a specified number of points higher. Tolls for characters not holding such cards do not increase.

A night's sleep

The character must gain a solid night's sleep in circumstances not much less safe and comfortable than they would be used to during their ordinary, non-mystery-investigating life.

Discard

Unless otherwise specified, the instruction 'discard' applies to the card the text appears on.

Nonlethal

Cannot be your Final card. If received when you are one short of the Final card in its category, you take the card and undergo its effects, if any, but your character does not leave play.

> You have 2 Injury cards in hand, in a game played in Terror mode. You receive the Tipsy Injury card, which is Nonlethal. Your character does not die.

However, a nonlethal card does count towards your total when you have it in hand already and another incoming card becomes your Final card.

> Later, after discarding one of your other Injury cards, you have 2 remaining: Breaking Point and Tipsy. You then get a third card, Ravaged by the Elements. In this instance Tipsy does count toward your total, and your character dies. You shouldn't have gone out into that blizzard half-tanked on brandy!

Recipient

When one character performs a test or spends to benefit another, the character receiving the benefit is the recipient. When a card says you must be the recipient of a success or spend to discard a card, your character may not perform the action; any other PC can.

HAZARDS

Dangers faced outside of combat are called hazards. Hazards can be physical or mental.

• • •

PHYSICAL HAZARDS

Physical hazards can be avoided, or their effects minimised, by making Athletics or Health tests.

Athletics tests apply when harm can be avoided with a quick dodge or other overt, intentional defensive action. Examples include:

- Falling from a great height.
- Ducking flying debris.
- Leaping out of the way of a
- plummeting object.
- Swimming in a dangerous current.
- Leaping over a chasm or between buildings.
- Rushing from a flaming building without getting burned.

Health tests happen in passive situations where you are exposed to a physical danger and the question that remains is how badly it affects you. This applies to instances of:

- Poisoning.
- Sickness.
- Exposure.

The GM may also call for Health tests when the character has had no chance to actively evade a danger that would otherwise call for an Athletics test. For example, if doused in kerosene and set alight while helpless, a Health test might determine whether the character suffers severe burns, or merely loses some hair and perhaps an eyebrow or two.

Each physical hazard threatens a Minor or a Major Injury, depending on the test result.

- On a success, the character does not take an Injury card.
- On a failure with a margin of 0 or 1, the character takes the Minor Injury card.
- On a failure by a margin of 2 or more, the character takes the Major Injury card.

Certain Injury cards gained from fights or hazards can be traded, under conditions specified in their text entries, for less punitive secondary cards.

PHYSICAL HAZARD TABLE

Situation	Difficulty	Ability	Minor Injury	Major Injury
Adder Strike	4	Athletics	Snakebit	Deadly Venom
Crushing Hazard	4	Athletics	Contused	Crushed
Drinking (Moderate)	4	Health	Tipsy	Drunk
Drowning	4	Athletics	Cough, Choke, Sputter	Lungful of Water
Escaping a Burning Building	4	Athletics	Singed	Burned
Exploding Bomb	4	Athletics	Thrown Free of the Explosion	In the Blast Radius
Flying Debris	4	Athletics	Something in Your Eye	Puncture Wound
Food Poisoning	4	Health	Stay by the Water Closet	Ructious Innards
Gunshot	4	Athletics	Grazed	Shot
Leap from Second Story Window	4	Athletics	Hard Landing	Turned Ankle
Rock Fall	4	Athletics	Abrasion	Concussed
Roughed up While Helpless	4	Health	It Looks Worse Than It Is	Broken Fingers
Sea Sickness	4	Healthy	Woozy	Nodens' Wrath
Toxin	4	Health	Mostly Resistant	Find the Antidote
Crushing Hazard	4	Athletics	Contused	Crushed
Angry Mob Set Upon You	5	Athletics	Black and Blue	Badly Beaten
Severe Exposure	5	Health	Warm Blanket Needed	Ravaged by the Elements
Smoke Inhalation	5	Health	Lingering Cough	Scarred Lungs
Tortured	5	Health	Through the Ringer	Breaking Point
Fall from a Great Height	7	Athletics	It's a Miracle You're Alive	Massive Injuries
Drinking (Heavy)	8	Health	Tipsy	Drunk

• • •

MENTAL HAZARDS

Mental hazards require characters to make Composure tests to attempt to avoid becoming victim to hallucinations, fear or a tortured psyche.

- On a success, the character does not take a Shock card.
- On a failure with a margin of 0 or 1, the character takes the Minor Shock card.
- On a failure with a margin of 2 or more, the character takes the Major Shock card.

MENTAL HAZARD TABLE

Situation	Difficulty	Minor Shock	Major Shock
You Badger a Vulnerable Witness	3	Overstepped Bounds	Wracked by Remorse
You Find Yourself Hemmed In	3	Oh Dear	Bit of a Sticky Wicket
You Hear a Disquieting Sound	3	Unnerved	Agitated
You Make a Fool of Yourself in Public	3	Embarrassed	Humiliated
Your Senses Deceive You (Or Do They?)	3	Uncertainty	Questioning Your Senses
Something's Not Quite Right	4	Unease	Dread
Things Go From Bad to Worse	4	Cause for Concern	Time to Panic
You Court Bad Luck	4	Jinx	Ill-Omened
You Enter a Foreboding Place	4	Foreboding Place	Terrible Place
You Have a Vision of Things to Come	4	Alarming Vision	Ghastly Vision
You See But Don't Interact with an Ancient/ Ghost	4	Rattled	I Need a Distraction
You Witness a Brutally Murdered Corpse	4	The Shudders	Shaken
You Gaze Upon the Otherworld	5	Glimpsed the Veil	Seeing the Great God Pan
You've Killed Someone	5	A Touch of the Shakes	An Image Seared into the Mind
You See a Great God's True Form	7	There's Something About Them	True Form

REGAINING PUSHES AND POOL POINTS

Spent points from various pools are restored at different rates, depending on their narrative purpose. Characters reset to 2 Pushes at the beginning of each new mystery. Most groups finish mysteries over one to three sessions. Players may revise their sense of how carefully to manage point spending as they see how quickly their group typically disposes of its cases.

General ability pools restore at the end of each mystery, or when a long break of world time uneventfully zips by in the course of a mystery. For example, if the group takes a long train ride to Cardiff, the time spent playing cards, hobnobbing with other passengers and having an all-important snooze allows for a full refresh of all pools. However, if they spend all their time on the train investigating why the train is getting emptier without them seeing anyone actually disembark, then it's not time to refresh just yet.

IMPROVING ABILITIES

At the conclusion of each mystery, each character gets 1 Improvement point.

Players can spend Improvement points right away, or save them and spend them at any time. To gain a new Investigative ability, a player spends 2 Improvement points and requests the approval of the player (if any) who received it as part of a starting kit. As GM you may waive this requirement if the latter player is frequently unable to attend game sessions.

Players may add points to a General ability, including those rated at 0, gaining 1 rating point for each Improvement point spent.

What Do Pool Points Represent?

Pool points are a literary abstraction, representing the way that characters get their own time in the spotlight in the course of an ensemble drama. When you do something remarkable, you expend a little bit of your spotlight time. More active players will spend their points sooner than less demonstrative ones, unless they carefully pick and choose their moments to shine.

Even when pools are empty, you still have a reasonable chance to succeed at a test, and you'll always get the information you need to move forward in the case.

Pool points do not represent a resource, tangible or otherwise, in the game world. Players are aware of them, but characters are not. The team members' ignorance of them is analogous to TV characters' obliviousness to commercial breaks, the unwritten rules of scene construction, and how there's usually a big reveal at the end of a season.

The characters do not literally get worse at doing things as the players expend points.

Instead, the players have used up their share of big spotlight moments they tied to their key abilities.

You may choose to depict this with narration – describing characters as drawn and exhausted when their Athletics pools ebb. But the system works just as well if you don't worry about matching literal description to an abstract resource.

CUSTOM INTERPERSONAL ABILITIES

Players can add custom Interpersonal abilities to the game as part of improvement. The player must explain how the ability helps the character gain cooperation from others, and give it a name that memorably sums it up.

CHARACTER REPLACEMENT

When you lose a character due to physical death or psychic breakdown, create a new one using the standard steps for character creation.

When choosing your Occupation Kit, pick any kit no other player is using. That could be the same one your previous character had, or one nobody picked. If you want, swap out any of those Investigative abilities for any other one available in the current campaign. Don't swap in more than one ability already possessed by another player's character.

SAFETY TOOLS

In horror roleplaying we collectively face our fears as part of the game. While this book sets out what is meant by weird folk horror, everyone has their own view of what horror is and their own psychological limits at the gaming table. Unlike a movie, roleplaying games are emergent, with no two sessions being the same so having a set of safety tools in place for everyone's peace of mind is a great idea. These aren't to get in the way of a game (after all, it's horror) but just having them as part of your playgroup can help. Therefore, safety tools are not only recommended, but should be used with every group that plays to ensure that players feel safe. There are several safety tools at your disposal, so use whatever your group agrees is best for them.

• • •

THE X-CARD

Set aside a piece of paper marked with an X. If a scene comes up that any player feels uncomfortable with, they can point to the X Card and the GM will either alter the scene or fade to black, picking up the story after the scene.

• • •

LINES AND VEILS

Before a game begins, have each player fill out a sheet of paper labelled with the headers 'lines' and 'veils'. Under 'lines' they should write anything they don't want to see in the game. Under 'veils' should be content that can be included but will occur off-screen, so to speak.

• • •

AGE RATINGS

Just as with a film, your group can settle on an age rating to communicate what content may be inappropriate. An 18-rated game would likely include graphic descriptions of horror while a PG rating would be implied or 'soft' horror. Machen mainly hinted at gore in his stories, instead building up dread as his tales progressed.

CLUES

All these are but dreams and shadows; the shadows that hide the real world from our eyes.

The Great God Pan

*T*he *Terror Beneath* is built on the wonderful framework provided by the GUMSHOE System, which allows players to really feel like investigators in their own horror mystery. A key part of this system is the **clue**: an element of the story that drives the investigation from one scene to the next. A clue can be anything worthy of note: a perfumed handkerchief, a half-burned letter, a matchbook or an overheard conversation between two lovers. It's up to the GM to sprinkle a variety of different clues throughout the mystery, all of which are discussed in this section.

GATHERING CLUES

Every *The Terror Beneath* mystery begins with a central question that forms the heart of an investigation. A question could be:

- Why did several climbers disappear in the mountains?
- What is creating those strange noises beneath The British Museum?
- Why is the underground train covered in black ichor?
- Who is hunting those Bright Young Things?
- How do we activate the magic in the standing stones?
- How has this Welsh village appeared from nowhere?

An investigation begins with the first question and builds through a series of scenes where characters discover new clues that lead them to a new scene. Sometimes they will miss a scene because they have a choice in which lead to follow next. This is good as it gives players autonomy and GMs should consider how they can improvise should the investigation take an unseen turn.

Gathering clues is simple. All you have to do is:

1. Get yourself into a scene where relevant information can be gathered.
2. Have the right ability to discover the clue.
3. Tell the GM that you're using it.

As long as you do these three things, you will never fail to gain a piece of necessary information. It is never dependent on a die roll. If you ask for it, you will get it.

You can specify exactly what you intend to achieve: 'I use Dérive to see if I recognise the architecture in this part of London.'

Or you can engage in a more general informational fishing expedition: 'I use Occultism to see if there's anything of occult interest in the area.'

If your suggested action corresponds to a clue in the mystery notes, the GM provides you the information arising from the clue.

The investigators are on the trail of a phantom hound in the heart of Brixton. Up to now, the clues have led them to the dingy cellar of a pub called the Fox and Hounds.

GM: 'There's a leather satchel sat on the floor, a book peeping out of the top.'

Player: 'I remove the book from the satchel and take a look.'

GM: 'The title is Lords of the Wild Hunt. There's an inscription in ink on the back cover, but the language is a series of strange sigils and lines.'

Player: 'I use my Linguistics ability to see if I can translate.'

GM: 'After a moment's study you understand this is written in the ancient Aklo language. The passage refers to the Horn of Annwn, reading: "The Horn of Annwn shall be sounded on the highest point".'

• • •

PASSIVE CLUES

Some clues would be obvious to a trained investigator immediately upon entering a scene. These **passive clues** are provided by the GM without prompting.

Player: 'Does the book look old?'

GM: 'You notice the pages of the book are foxed and yellowed, almost crumbling to the touch. It's very likely over a century old, but the ink appears much more recent.'

Mysteries suggest which clues are passive and which are active, but your GM will adjust these in play depending on how much guidance you seem to need. On a night when you're cooking with gas, the GM will sit back and let you prompt them for passive clues. When you're bogged down, they may volunteer what would normally be active clues.

GM: 'You pull out an old book entitled Lords of the Wild Hunt. Opening it up you see strange writing in ink on the back cover. Does anyone have Linguistics?'

Player: 'I do.'

GM: 'Perfect. You recognise the writing as ancient Aklo. The passage refers to the Horn of Annwn, reading: "The Horn of Annwn shall be sounded on the highest point".'

• • •

CORE CLUES

For each scene, the GM designates a **core clue**. This is the clue you absolutely need to move to the next scene, and thus to complete the entire investigation. GMs will avoid making core clues available only with the use of obscure Investigative abilities. (For that matter, the character creation system is set up so that the group as a whole will have access to all, or nearly all, of these abilities.) The ability the GM designates is just one possibility, not a straitjacket – if players come up with another plausible method, the GM should give out the information.

• • •

INCONSPICUOUS CLUES

Sometimes the characters instinctively notice something without actively looking for it. Often this situation occurs in places they're moving through casually and don't regard as scenes in need of intensive searching. The team might pass by a concealed door, spot a droplet of blood on the marble of an immaculate hotel lobby or approach a vehicle with a bomb planted beneath it. Interpersonal abilities can also be used to find **inconspicuous clues**. The classic example is of a character whose demeanour or behavioural tics establish them as suspicious.

It's unreasonable to expect players to ask to use their various abilities in what appears to be an innocuous transitional scene.

Otherwise, they'd have to spend minutes of game time with every change of scene, running down their abilities in obsessive checklist fashion.

Instead, the GM asks which character has the highest current pool in the ability in question.

If two or more pools are equal, it goes to the one with the highest rating. If ratings are also equal, their characters find the clue at the same time.

• • •

SIMPLE SEARCHES

Many clues can be found without any ability whatsoever. If an ordinary person could credibly find a clue simply by looking in a specified place, the clue discovery occurs automatically. You, the reader, wouldn't need to be a trained investigator to find a bloody footprint on the carpet in your living room, or notice a manila envelope taped to the underside of a table at the local pub. By that same logic, the investigators don't require specific abilities to find them, either. When players specify that they're searching an area for clues, they're performing what we call a **simple search**.

Vary the way you run simple searches according to pacing needs and the preferences of your group. Some players like to feel that their characters are interacting with the imaginary environment. To suit them, use a call-and-response format, describing the scene in a way that suggests places to look. The player prompts back by zeroing in on a detail, at which point you reveal the clue:

> **GM:** 'Beside the window stands a roll-top desk.'
> **Player:** 'I look inside!'
> **GM:** 'You find an album full of old photographs.'

At other times, or for players less interested in these small moments of discovery, you might cut straight to the chase:

GM: 'You find an album full of old photographs in the roll-top desk.'

In the first case, the player who first voices interest in the detail finds the clue. In the second, it goes to, at your discretion:

- The character to whom the clue seems most thematically suited (for example, if you've established as a running motif that Christopher always stumbles on the disgusting clues, and this clue is disgusting, tell his player that he's once again stepped in it); or
- A player who hasn't had a win or spotlight time for a while.

• • •

LEVERAGED AND PREREQUISITE CLUES

A staple element of mystery writing is the crucial fact which, when presented to a previously resistant witness or suspect, causes him to break down and suddenly supply the information or confession the investigators seek. This is represented in GUMSHOE by the **leveraged clue**. This is a piece of information which is only available from the combined use of an Interpersonal ability, and the mention of another, previously gathered clue. The cited clue is called a **prerequisite clue**, and is by definition a sub-category of core clue. These often appear in different scenes.

> Earlier in the mystery, Jerome uses Essayist to discover that Martin Brightman, the famed *Tatler* columnist, is using a pen name to write sordid occult tales for the pulp magazine *Spicy Ghost*. The players suspect Brightman of having ties to a secret society who perform ritual sacrifice. They decide this would be good leverage against the journalist to get him to give them further information about the society. Later in the investigation, Seeta uses Society when interviewing Brightman to determine how much his standing among the literati would fall if his alter-ego were revealed. In desperation, Brightman agrees to give them an address for the society's meeting place.

PIPE CLUES

A clue which is important to the solution of the mystery, but which becomes significant much later in the mystery, is called a **pipe clue**. The name is a reference to screenwriting jargon, where the insertion of exposition that becomes relevant later in the narrative is referred to as 'laying pipe'. The term likens the careful arrangement of narrative information to the work performed by a plumber in building a house.

Pipe clues create a sense of structural variety in a mystery, lessening the sense that the PCs are being led in a strictly linear manner from Scene A to Scene B to Scene C. When they work well, they give players a 'eureka' moment, as they suddenly piece together disparate pieces of the puzzle. A possible risk with pipe clues lies in the possible weakness of player memories, especially over the course of a mystery broken into several sessions. The GM may occasionally have to prompt players to remember the first piece of a pipe clue when they encounter a later component.

> Victoria discovers a black mirror early on in the investigation, but with no context of who it belonged to and only a vague notion of how it would be used. Later on in the mystery, it transpires that a member of the Dee Society is using black mirrors to attempt to contact the so-called 'angels' (actually a group of soul-draining jeelo) to do her bidding.

THE LONDON METROPOLIS

All London was one grey temple of an awful rite, ring within ring of wizard stones circled about some central place, every circle was an initiation, every initiation eternal loss.

The Hill of Dreams

London is a dreamscape born from the banks of the River Thames, a sprawling forest of buildings whose shadows play host to a cocktail of mundane deviance and occult mystery. The Industrial Revolution caused the capital to rupture like a spleen, its contents spilling far beyond its previous boundaries as rural workers from ailing farmsteads came to secure their future. Greater London continued to expand, with 67,000 people arriving each year from 1901 to 1911 as its middle class grew in the newly created suburbs. By the breakout of the Great War in 1914, London was home to over seven million inhabitants: larger than the combined populations of Paris, Vienna and Saint Petersburg. Workers from Europe arrived in their droves, while the chance to be a part of the beating heart of the world's economy was a seductive prospect for those from the United States of America. In their new home these foreign workers found a vastly divided city where the poor were trampled in the muck and the elite would skirt any scandal if enough money were passed under the table. This was a metropolis where life reached its heady heights for some, while at the same time the worst conceivable fates awaited others. London is the architectural manifestation of life and death, good and evil.

THE IMPACT OF THE GREAT WAR

At the end of the war in 1918, nearly a million British soldiers lay dead on European battlefields, with more than two million disabled and in need of medical treatment. For London, the war had been an under-reported event. Unlike Paris, which had been on the front lines of the battle and subject to various bomb raids, or Saint Petersburg where revolution erupted, London life wasn't upturned in the same way. But London's need for labour in the war years led to a need for workers for shipbuilding, munitions and other wartime manufacturing.

While labourers toiled in factories under inhuman conditions, the British government dreamt up new machines of slaughter to deploy on the front lines. Their weapons and ordnance had to be faster and cheaper to create, but more lethal. Scientists were brought in to test new technologies, such as mustard gas (tested by Martha Whitely of Imperial College London) and more experimental techniques of empowering the troops overseas.

THE WEIRD OFFICE

Many of these secretive experiments were carried out by the newly formed Ministry of Experimental Innovation, an offshoot of the Ministry of Munitions, whose experts had unorthodox ideas as to how Britain could prevail in the war. A nickname given to the Ministry by insiders was the Weird Office for this reason, Shadowy science that blended cutting-edge technology and occult sorcery was carried out in the ministry's underground laboratories. Researchers used ritual magic set out by the likes of John Dee to communicate with what they believed to be angels, receiving supposedly divine information to help uncover enemy plans through black mirrors. Several weeks after making contact with these beings, those involved were found with their eyes clawed out by their own hands. At precisely the same time, soldiers in the trenches reported being aided by angelic figures in no-man's land. In another tragic event, two scientists were studying a possible passage into the Otherworld where it was theorised a new chemical weapon could be harvested. Through an experiment of vapour electrolysis, they managed to open the Veil only to unleash a phantom hound who tore them limb from limb. For each of these strange and bloody occurrences, the Ministry fed the media lies about new serial killers, gassers and poisoners. There were so many incidents that the Department of Truth was set up just to ensure these secret experiments were kept under wraps and out of the enemy's sight.

After the war ended, the Ministry of Experimental Innovation was officially shuttered, but unofficially a small group existed to continue its work in the eventuality of another global catastrophe: the Office of Otherworldly Matters (OOM).

POST-WAR LIFE IN LONDON

LONDON UNBOUND

Britain entered an era of prosperity in the 1920s as the war machine lined the pockets of traders and manufacturers. New industries such as motor vehicles, communications and chemicals led to an expansion in housing around Greater London. Aristocrats became more wealthy and Bright Young Things celebrated their new-found freedom throwing lavish parties, no expense spared. Women, who had been a key part of the war effort at home and abroad, had greater freedoms than ever before with the right to vote given to over 30s and the first birth control clinic being opened by Dr Marie Stopes in 1921.

• • •

A NEW TRANSPORT

Londoners were now more mobile, with the rise of the motor car allowing people to travel privately and in comfort. While cars were only affordable to the wealthy during the early part of the decade, later on prices dropped considerably meaning a small car could be bought for £300. A burgeoning middle class could now travel to the seaside for a day trip, leading to a local tourism boom as more people escaped the city for the beach. Congestion became a problem in the city and by 1928 traffic lights and roundabouts appeared and standardised road signs were installed across the country. While private vehicles were becoming more popular, the already established London Underground added new trains and started expanding lines into the new suburbs.

• • •

HOME AND ENTERTAINMENT

In the household, families could buy a comparatively expensive radio licence, listening to the newly established British Broadcasting Company from 1922 with its daily news bulletins and popular music programmes. American jazz was incredibly popular, causing a stir on the airwaves as well as the dancefloor as London nightclubs became the place to be. The arrival of the Charleston had an unprecedented impact on British culture, with 'flappers' becoming all the rage in the dance hall.

While the music had people flocking to smoky jazz clubs, the Picture Palace drew the crowds to catch the latest cinematic imports from Hollywood. These art deco celluloid temples showed the latest silent movies, turning actors such as Charlie Chaplin into overnight sensations.

LONDON'S OCCULT UNDERBELLY

The occult veins of London run deep, quietly meandering from the murder-haunted slums of Whitechapel to the distinguished offices of Parliament. History and folklore have built up over thousands of years since the Romans established Londinium, creating a city where every street is awash with lingering magic, attracting magical scholars from John Dee to Aleister Crowley. Vast hidden libraries of occult texts can be found if one knows where to look: some more dangerous than others.

• • •

THE ARCANIUS

If the British Library is the sum of all great knowledge, the Arcanius is the British Library of occult tomes. Set up by John Dee and Edward Kelley in 1584 to house the great works of magical literature, the Arcanius is accessed through a secret doorway in the Tower of London, descending into a grand hall filled with towering book cases. Only members of the Uriel Society can set foot in the library and study its texts, although a few exceptions have been made throughout the centuries. There are rumours of a great obsidian mirror within one of the library's chambers whose powers can communicate with beings from the Otherworld.

• • •

OCCULT SHOPS

The dark streets of London are punctuated with creaky little stores that sell all manner of occult paraphernalia, from tarot cards to forbidden tomes. The most frequented shops include Pan's Grove, The Fool's Emporium and John Black's. While most are more likely to carry trinkets with very little real power, some owners are members of secret societies with access to knowledge beyond human ken.

• • •

THE HOUSE OF HIDDEN LIGHT

If a magus were to frequent a local watering hole and discuss their business openly there would be outcry among the patrons that could warrant police involvement. Therefore, the magus Esmerelda Hollinsworth established The House of Hidden Light, a public house hidden except to those who walk magical paths. The door to the House shifts nightly, only revealed when the right spell is activated. Within is a dim den clouded in opium, cushions spread along the floor and ghastly leather books piled high. Paper lanterns hang from the ceiling emitting an intoxicating aroma of lavender and sandalwood. Anyone who is anyone in the occult world can likely be found here, drinking a brandy and smoking a pipe.

• • •

THE VEILED MARKET

The rare and special items that can't be found in one of London's occult shops can surely be discovered in the enigmatic Veiled Market. Squeezed within an alley in Bermondsey, close to St Mary Magdalene Churchyard, this strange marketplace exists only after midnight for an hour during the Hunter's Moon in October. Here hedge-mages and aristocratic magi rub shoulders to bid on objects of occult provenance. It is said that in 1845 Excalibur's scabbard was bought by an anonymous visitor, and in 1900 a Balor's eye was acquired by a Member of Parliament who has since passed away.

• • •

THE LIMEHOUSE PYRAMID

Located in the grounds of St Anne's Churchyard is a nine-foot-tall white pyramid inscribed with 'The Wisdom of Solomon' in both Hebrew and English. Who put the pyramid here and why remains a mystery, but a review of the Scarlet Map reveals the structure is at the intersection of several Veins and therefore a location of Bleed, which attracts a number of occult practitioners on a frequent basis to work their magic.

SECRET SOCIETIES OF LONDON

Machen's work is laced with secret societies, though none are laid out in detail. London has spawned many cults and occult organisations since its Roman inception, most of which operate hidden from the eyes of the general public. These societies are largely collectives of the London elite: those who have power and influence over the city, making them a dangerous force to be reckoned with and almost impossible to snuff out fully.

THE LOST CLUB

One of the most enigmatic societies in London, the Lost Club seems like any cosy club save that it exists independent of space. Members meet at a great, grim house in the vicinity of Fitzrovia, yet arriving there is often left to chance unless you know exactly where to look. Most of the time the house is a billiard table factory, but on certain nights throughout the year the Lost Club manifests within the building. Even stranger is the fact that aristocrats who are thought to be abroad have been noted as attending the club at the time of their absence from the country. At a given time of the night, members are invited to circle a grand table in a room with two exits. The club's chief, usually a member of the royal family, reads names from a large tome. Should they turn to the black page and read your name you are led through one of the doors and never seen again. The purpose of this rite is a mystery and where those poor members disappear off to nobody knows.

THE CULT OF DIONYSUS

For some, Dionysus is a classical god relegated to paintings and sculptures. But for his cult, Dionysus is the writhing god of the vineyard who promises animalistic ecstasy through the drinking of the blasphemous wine bakkheia. His followers place hedonism above all other philosophies, carrying out the sacred imbibing rite that causes their hideous transformation into raving beast-people who dance by the moonlight. Cult leaders maintain hidden vineyards producing the bitter bakkheia grape, tainted by the blood of sacrificed bulls, goats and horses to craft their doom-wine. The wine is then sold to shadowy dealers in London at underground markets for prices that only the gentry could afford. After the war, the Cult of Dionysus has become popular with some Bright Young Things who crave new and more dangerous excesses.

THE URIEL SOCIETY

John Dee's contributions to the occult echoed throughout the British Empire, an idea he was in part responsible for. One of his greatest works was the creation of the vast obsidian speculum used to contact Otherworldly beings he considered to be angels. Centuries after his death, a group called the Uriel Society formed around his ideas and became caretakers of the Arcanius. Members wear the garb of the sixteenth-century elite and their language is as archaic as their attire. The Uriel Society don't believe their intentions to harness the power of the 'angels' are sinister. After all, who were the mysterious ethereal bowmen who appeared over Mons and saved their troops if not angels directly summoned by the society? Dee believed the Otherworld to be heaven and its inhabitants were servants of the Lord who would come to heal us in our time of need. He never suspected that through his communications with these beings he was inadvertently thinning the Veil around London to nearly cataclysmic degrees.

• • •

THE WORMWOOD CLUB

Hidden in the depths of Soho in an unmarked building is a club where patrons hope to gain a glimpse into the Otherworld. Lady Warton, who founded the club in 1913, has mastered the synthesis of the most exquisite absinthe with the sap of a certain willow tree that grows near the ancient cairns in Gwynedd, Wales. A sip of this radiant elixir induces a trance-state where the mundane smokescreen of our world evaporates, and in its place appears a vista beyond mortal reckoning where the old gods squirm. It is true that some go mad from the revelation, though most believe the experience to be a mere trick of the mind brought on by the unique properties of the drink.

• • •

ALPHA ET OMEGA

At the end of the century, the Hermetic Order of the Golden Dawn had become fractured, giving rise to several offshoots, including Alpha et Omega (abbreviated A.O) founded by Samuel Liddell MacGregor Mathers in 1888. The secret society continued Golden Dawn's mission to achieve spiritual development through magical means such as astral travel, divination, scrying and alchemy. The temple is located on Blythe Road, Kensington, named Isis-Urania, where members study the 60 mystical Cipher Manuscripts that dictate the beliefs and structure of the organisation. It is their belief that magic is the only way to attain the perfect self and this can only be achieved through their works that draw on the power of the Otherworld so that they themselves can become divine beings. Notable members of A.O included Bram Stoker, Sir Arthur Conan Doyle, W.B. Yeats and a certain Arthur Machen.

• • •

THE KNIGHTS TEMPLAR

The Templar has a long and storied history dating back to the time of the Crusades. The French knight Hugues de Payens formed the Poor Fellow-Soldiers of Christ and the Temple of Solomon in the twelfth century, which would later become the Knights Templar. At that time the order was incredibly wealthy, even lending money to kings to finance their wars. It wasn't until

Pope Clement V dissolved the Knights Templar in 1312, and redistributed their wealth, that the secret society was created. The Knights were created with a higher purpose, one that they kept under wraps for centuries: they were on the hunt for the Grail. Their leaders were believed to have received a vision from King Arthur himself who tasked them with this most holy of quests. Now the Knights Templar meet within the halls of government, royalty and academia to further their search through means less virtuous than Arthur intended. Now the order believes the Grail to lie not within our physical reality but in a place beyond: the Otherworld.

THE CULT OF VENUS

The Roman goddess of beauty, desire and prosperity has taken many forms in many cults throughout the centuries. Romantic depictions of Venus bely her true nature as a dark goddess whose powers of manipulation are craved by her mortal worshippers. Only the most beautiful people are sacrificed to Venus, in exchange for the gift of desire and influence over others. This gift makes the cult a popular choice for all classes of society who seek control to get what they want in life.

THE WELSH WILDERNESS

He loved to meditate on a land laid waste, Britain deserted by the legions, the rare pavements riven by frost, Celtic magic still brooding on the wild hills and in the black depths of the forest, the rosy marbles stained with rain, and the walls growing grey.

The Hill of Dreams

Far away from the palpable energy of the capital loom the dark hills of the Welsh countryside, a landscape reeking with Otherwordly magic, where forgotten creatures of ancient times crawl madly through the suffocating woodlands. The bucolic paintings by Lewis, Walters and Cotman defy the true terror of Wales' fields, moors and valleys. This land remembers the time before time, its memory imbued in imposing standing stones whose cold faces witnessed the ritual slaughter of kinfolk. Cairns erected to petty kings and cursed by cunning women dot the landscape, beneath which slither great black corpse-eating serpents. Within the mountains, vast caves are the breeding grounds for things that squirm and bite, beings the locals call the 'fair folk' or 'tylwyth teg'. Villagers whose ways may seem quaint, even simple, to the London elite, conceal long-forgotten knowledge of the stones, the hills, the woods and all they hold. They steer clear of the strange lights floating in the marshlands and their pockets bulge with rowan berries to stave off the wee folk. Outsiders are warned to keep to the trail and not to venture out in the darkness without a guide for, they say, the shadows move strangely in these parts. It is in these places where Celtic shamans trod that the Veil is at its strongest. One glance of the Scarlet Map quickly reveals the Welsh country to be one crimson mass of criss-crossed lines and deep inky spots where Bleed pours from the Otherworld. This is the stronghold of the Great Gods, and they are wrathful.

THE IMPACT OF THE GREAT WAR

Nearly 11 percent of the Welsh population enlisted in the war effort between 1914 and Armistice Day in 1918. The cost of lives abroad and at home was devastating as communities were fractured.

Coal mining played a vital role in Welsh life, supporting the economy which saw a boom during the war due to demand for fuel. At its peak, the South Wales Coalfield was one of the largest in the world, but the move towards oil as a fuel source for ships and rapid overexpansion led to the decline of coal mining. Pit closures foretold the oncoming depression, seeing 28.5 percent of coal miners unemployed by August 1924. The industrial growth enjoyed by Wales in the century beforehand had been snatched away all within a decade as small holders and farmers faced stark hardships in rural areas. With this the landed gentry, who relied on farming to salt their coffers, crumbled. Even the Church was impacted by a move away from organised religion towards secularism and, more prevalently in rural areas, embracing the old gods of the Romans and Celts. Hard-bitten communities became more insular to outsiders keeping their seemingly odd ways to themselves.

PLACES OF POWER IN RURAL WALES

If you were to explore the Roman ruins of Caerleon, move through the towering stones of Pentre Ifan or traverse the ancient woodland of Coed Felenrhyd & Llennyrch, you would feel a tingle darting up the back of your neck as you travelled a land where the Otherworld and ours meet. These are Places of Power, locations saturated with Bleed. Here ancient ones move in shadows and black ceremonies are enacted under the pallid moon.

• • •

THE LLANGERNYW YEW (CONWY)

At over 4,000 years old this venerable tree is the oldest living tree in Wales. In its infancy it stood at the birth of Stonehenge during Europe's Neolithic Age and watched empires rise and fall. The Celts venerated the tree as a sign of rebirth due to the yew's ability to regrow after death. It is believed a spirit called the Angelystor resides within the tree and on the night of All Hallows' Eve will whisper the names of locals due to die within the year. At midnight parishioners around the village gather to listen to the Angelystor, despite protests from the local vicar who believes the creature to be a demon. Those whose names are spoken are marked and shunned, believed to be an ill omen for whoever they speak with.

• • •

TINKINSWOOD (VALE OF GLAMORGAN)

Tinkinswood burial chamber is a megalithic dolmen – an ancient tomb topped with a 40-tonne capstone. The chamber was excavated in 1914, where archaeologists unearthed over 900 smashed human bones. They were baffled by what they saw, as the bones seemed to have been crushed by a large set of knife-like teeth. Even stranger was evidence of an old tunnel seemingly dug beneath the dolmen spanning for miles. Locals believe that spending the night near Tinkinswood leads to madness or divine knowledge, but few have the stomach to test the theory.

• • •

FFOS ANNODUN (BETWS-Y-COED)

Colloquially known as the Fairy Glen, this secluded gorge is said to be home to the tylwyth teg. The old saying goes that one must 'wait and wait to see the fairy men' and that only the most patient would catch a glimpse of the wee folk who prowl here. Those who live closer to the woodland never cross the gorge in the dark and keep flaming lanterns on them at all times, in case the 'fairies come out to play'. It's not uncommon for children to go missing in the gorge, only to return days later with a complete change of personality and a glassy look in their eyes.

• • •

PENTRE IFAN (PEMBROKESHIRE)

God does not follow one to Pentre Ifan, the folks say over their beer mug. Framed by the gloomy Preseli Hills, Pentre Ifan is a large Neolithic stone chamber that has existed for around 5,000 years. The three towering uprights supporting the huge capstone resemble a large doorway. It is here that the Veil is thin and Bleed pulsates through the air as this is indeed a doorway to the Otherworld, albeit one that requires activation through blasphemous ritual. The voor have been known to drag people through the archway, never to be seen again. When the moon is full, one can hear a foul dirge on the breeze played by the voor pipers beyond the dimensional gateway. In 1913, the Weird Office sent two agents through the gate after performing a sacrifice. They returned in mad panic from what they had seen and were unable to speak another word.

• • •

BRYN CELLI DDU (ISLE OF ANGLESEY)

In English the name of this Neolithic tomb translates to 'Mound in the Dark Grove'. Entering through the passage one finds themselves in a circular chamber crafted from blueschist rock faintly patterned with the strange shapes of the ancient Welsh. It is customary for visitors to make an offering to the dead, usually of bone, feather or coin. Those who leave without partaking in the ritual will be followed home by a gwyllon.

• • •

COED FELENRHYD & LLENNYRCH (SNOWDONIA)

This ancient Celtic rainforest spans over 700 acres and has become popular with ramblers from the city who venture out for the day to walk in these wild, moss-covered woods. During the spring and summer, the woodland is beautiful, with echoes of birdsong and the rustle of animals in the undergrowth hunting for nuts and berries. But in the winter, the beauty gives way to horror as the woods are transformed into a cathedral of grey mist and wandering shadows. Those who live close by speak of the corpse birds whose sightings are portents of death, or the witch-rites that occur deep in the night.

• • •

ROMAN FORTRESS OF *ISCA AUGUSTA* (CAERLEON)

The remains of a Roman fort complete with a wall, amphitheatre and barracks can be found in Caerleon. Here audiences would watch bloody gladiatorial battles and gaze upon the strange creatures captured in distant lands. One can almost hear the shouts and cries of slain warriors on the wind and smell the sweat of the barracks. In 1915, the Weird Office believed the resonant energy of battle that lingered in the environment could be harnessed for the war effort. So began the experiment codenamed 'Legion', where enlisted soldiers would be subject to a possession ritual. When one lad turned into a rage-filled murderer who slew three scientists and a government agent with a piece of slate the experiment was shut down, but the soldier was never found again.

• • •

TWMBARLWM (GWENT)

The so-called 'Hill of Dreams' is surrounded by a vast aura of Bleed. Said to be the final resting place of mythical Welsh king Bran the Blessed, the hill is a convergence between the Otherworld and ours. To stand on Twmbarlwm is to be in the presence of the ancient ones and the druids who once cavorted here making sacrifices to their gods. Echoes of their voices and strange piping can still be heard when the wind blows just right. Ghostly visions of sinister sacrifice have been witnessed on the hill and many a child that has climbed to its peak has never been seen again.

CAERWENT (GWENT)

Caerwent boasts the ruins of a Roman settlement in which stood a great temple to Nodens. Stone reliefs depicting strange fish-tailed beings were recently excavated and a hidden series of chambers beneath the ground discovered by Professor Artemis Wishaw of the University of Cambridge. Wishaw and his students spent ten days working in the darkness below, unearthing ritual daggers and a tablet of incantations called the Codex Nodens. When they emerged, many of the students wouldn't speak of some of the objects they found and Wishaw himself sat for months in the darkness of his chamber muttering about the god beneath the waves. One student who managed to keep her wits explained how something had spoken to them in the ruins of that temple, telling them awful things that nobody should know. Later the government sealed the entrance to the ruin and posted military personnel in the area to prevent trespassing.

PAGAN CULTS OF THE WILDS

It's in the quietest corners of the country where evil plants it roots, growing like insidious knotweed, ensnaring the desperate, depraved and damaged. Usually the evil presents itself as an innocuous tradition, like a corn doll hanging in the window or a merry dance around the orchard. But then it gently creeps in: animal sacrifice, kidnappings, murder. Impoverished communities put their hopes in beings ancient and terrible. Their prayers are answered in blood and agony. The crops flourish. Their economy returns. So the cycle continues until all are enraptured by the Otherworld. Cults spring up all around Wales, acting in the interests of the Great Gods, pushing forward their agenda to once again reclaim the mortal world.

• • •

THE CHILDREN OF PAN

Pan, the Lord of the Wilds, is a powerful figure among the foothills and mountains of Wales. Those who worship him are called his Children. These are often livestock owners who venerate Pan's goat aspect, praying for their animals' safety during the harsh winter months when death is an all-too-common reality. Their chapels are grottoes formed in the mountains, where stone depictions of the horned being are kissed and fondled in the hope he will send a blessing. His priests are Pan-born abominations: spawn of a tryst with the god and a mortal. They play awful screeching symphonies on their blackened flutes as the congregation dances madly before a human sacrifice is made to appease their lord.

• • •

THE MANDRAKE

Witch cults have survived for centuries in the Welsh hills, avoiding the witch hunts of the Medieval and Renaissance periods. While so many innocent people over the centuries were put to death under the auspices of religious piety, the real evil hid in the shadows performing their sinister rites around standing stones. While some lurked away in nature, others lived under the very nose of civilisation: the estate nanny, the village baker, the quiet librarian. The Mandrake is one such witch cult who uses its emerging powers as a conduit for the Otherworld. Its members secretly induct the young through the teachings of seemingly harmless folk magic, until one day they must sign the Black Book and give their names to the Dark Lord. While

most believe this to be the Devil, in reality their worship is directed towards Pan, whose image as a horned goat-like entity has become misconstrued as the Christian Satan.

• • •

CULT OF THE HOLLOW ONES

Small mining communities were hit hard by the economy's collapse in the wake of the war. Mines were shut and mining families were left to starve. Yet some ex-miners discovered a strange truth hidden deep in the mines. Some called them 'knockers' and others referred to them as the Hollow Ones: small, troglodytic voor who lived in the mine shafts. The miners greatly feared the Hollow Ones, whose round eyes burned in the darkness and whose red tongues licked bloody teeth. But belief soon grew that the creatures were little gods who should be appeased by offering living sacrifices. In turn, the Hollow Ones would ensure the community's livestock was never threatened by predators and outsiders would stay away from their homes. Each new moon a sacrifice would be selected by lottery and given to the ravenous beings who would drag them into the darkness. When people from elsewhere found themselves in one of these communities there would be no lottery. In at least one community, a missed sacrifice has led to the voor crawling from the pits in the night and taking their fill of human life.

• • •

LORDS OF THE WILD HUNT

The blasting of a ram's horn and the beat of sheepskin drums signify the coming of the Wild Hunt. Cloaked figures bedecked in mossy antlers and flanked by baying spectral hounds descend on villages whose windows and doors have been boarded up for just this occasion. The hounds of Annwn seek out souls for Arawn, while their human guides tear people from their bedsides and into the streets, tears streaming down their faces. It is customary at this time for village folk to mark Celtic warding signs on their doors and cast spells on their thresholds to keep the hounds at bay.

• • •

THE SERPENT'S EYE

Something terrible squirms beneath the earth. A giant corpse-eating snake, swollen and glutted, writhes below the cairns and dolmens of the Black Mountains. Known to some as the Low King, the Black Serpent of the Cairn is viewed by its cult of worshippers as the God of the Black Mountains. They who call themselves The Serpent's Eye believe the Low King is due to rise into the world and devour all sinners

in its magnificent maw while its devotees inherit a new heaven ruled by their dark deity. Therefore, the Black Serpent of the Cairn must be fed. Always.

• • •

PEOPLE OF THE LAKE

Most wealthy landowners and estate holders were ruined in the mid-1920s. Those once used to a lavish lifestyle in white-pillared manor houses were now forced to sell up or face destitution. One desperate landowner in Conwy discovered a lake beneath her home inhabited by a race of silver-skinned nymphs. Central to the subterranean lake was a marble statue of the god Nodens, the great and terrible god of oceans. The landowner was told by the nymphs that treasure she gave to them would be returned tenfold. She soon realised that they didn't mean literal treasure, but people she loved. First her cousin met an abrupt end before being thrown into the lake. Then her aunt, uncle and afterwards her husband met their fates as sacrifices to Nodens. She became wealthy once more and extended her estate, incorporating imagery of Nodens and the nymphs into the architecture. Other landowners asked what her secret was and, running low on sacrifices, she divulged information about her new god. Though initially horrified, others brought the people they treasured down to the lake and drowned them in the darkness. After several months a rich community who called themselves the People of the Lake began to flourish, all the while on the prowl for their next victim.

FORBIDDEN SORCERY

> It appears to me that it is simply an attempt to penetrate into another and higher sphere in a forbidden manner. You can understand why it is so rare. They are few, indeed, who wish to penetrate into higher spheres, higher or lower, in ways allowed or forbidden.
>
> *The White People*

In the Machenesque milieu, sorcery is rarely the star of the story but hangs like an ominous cloud over the horror that unfolds before our investigator heroes. There are never powerful wizards casting mighty fireballs, but there is a quiet malign magic that hints at the ancient evils of the Otherworld. In *The White People*, the young girl's nurse slowly indoctrinates her into folk magic practices, and in *The Inmost Light* there are clear occult practices involved in trapping Dr Black's wife in the stone. Such magic isn't carried out by the good guys, so it's rare that the investigators in *The Terror Beneath* should be using foul sorcery. Yet there are desperate times that call for the uttering of the unutterable from a tattered grimoire or Neolithic tablet.

SORCERY TESTS

Casting a spell, whether reading from a grimoire or creating a clay poppet, requires the caster to roll a Composure test with the Difficulty determined by the spell at hand. Passing the Composure test means the caster has maintained a sound mind. Failing means that the spell not only fails to work, but has serious physical or psychological effects on the caster. The caster takes a Major Shock card. It should be noted that most powerful spells are incredibly difficult to pull off, which is why it's often easier to approach sorcery as a group (though this is by no means a walk in the park).

SORCERY TOLLS

With more complex and dangerous spells, passing a Composure test still sometimes means taking a Toll, which is deducted from Athletics, Fighting or Health. If the caster can't afford to pay a Toll or doesn't wish to, they instead take a Major Shock card.

• • •

GROUP SORCERY TESTS

Pulling together as a group to cast a spell can help share the burden of using sorcery. Any number of investigators can help with a spell that has a Toll cost of 2 or more. Assign a lead caster to roll the Composure test to cast the spell. If those aiding the lead spend 1 Composure, the lead gets a +1 to the roll, but every helper must spend 1 for the lead to get this bonus. If passed, the investigators can divide the Toll among themselves. However, on a fail they each must take a Shock card. In a group test, this Shock card may be avoided by spending a Push. Some spells are made more effective by the amount of Composure spent when casting, so group tests can be a good way to achieve this.

BLEED REQUIREMENTS

In some cases, more powerful spells require a certain amount of Bleed in a location to cast properly. The spell description lists the amount of Bleed required to cast. If the spell is cast in a location where Bleed is lower, the caster takes a -1 to the Composure roll for every Bleed level they are away from the required level, thus making it more likely they will take a Shock card. For example, casting a spell that needs a Bleed 3 in a location of Bleed 1 would mean the caster taking a -2 to their Composure roll. This means that attempting to summon the avatar of a Great God in an area of low Bleed is almost guaranteed to lead to the caster's soul becoming corrupted.

• • •

TIME

Every spell description lists the time taken to cast. This time must be unbroken, otherwise the spell won't work.

• • •

SPELL FOCI

Spell foci are rare items that can aid in the casting process. Often these foci take the shape of legendary objects such as the Holy Grail, Excalibur or Merlin's staff. When casting a spell using a focus, gain +2 to the Composure test. If making a sorcery test with a group, the leader must be the one wielding the focus. If the spell is successful the focus will become inert and unusable for a time determined by the GM. This could be a matter of hours but could even span months or years.

SPELLS

Augury

A spell cast to divine the future using an obsidian mirror. The GM determines a core clue that the investigators have yet to find to appear in the mirror.

Difficulty: 6
Bleed Required: 2
Toll: 2
Casting Time: 10 minutes
Major Shock: Ghastly Vision

Banish Ancient/Otherworld Being

The spell allows the caster to send an ancient or being from the Otherworld (that isn't a Great God) back to the Otherworld. The being must be in the vicinity of the caster for the spell to work.

Difficulty: 5
Bleed Required: 1
Toll: 3
Casting Time: 1 minute
Major Shock: Seeing the Great God Pan

Banish Great God Avatar

A powerful sorcery that opens a tunnel to the Otherworld and forcibly pushes a Great God's avatar through before instantly closing. The avatar must be in the vicinity of the caster for the spell to work.

Difficulty: 7
Bleed Required: 3
Toll: 4
Casting Time: 5 minutes
Major Shock: Seeing the Great God Pan

Bind Great God Avatar

Once the avatar of a Great God has been summoned to the mortal world it can be bound with this spell. While bound, the avatar is unable to move away from the binding location, which is usually a salt circle on the ground or possibly an entire room whose exits are thoroughly warded. The avatar is bound indefinitely or until the binding is broken by a spell.

Difficulty: 7
Bleed Required: 3
Toll: 4
Casting Time: 10 minutes
Major Shock: Mind's Agony

Bleed Surge

This spell is designed to increase the Bleed in a location by 1. This is usually performed at the site of a Vein. The maximum Bleed that can be achieved is 3.

Difficulty: 5
Bleed Required: 1
Toll: 1
Casting Time: 1 hour
Major Shock: Mind's Agony

Far Sight

The caster is able to see events unfolding in the present at a location other than their own. They must have visited this location previously for the spell to work.

Difficulty: 4
Bleed Required: 1
Toll: 1
Casting Time: 1 minute
Major Shock: Ghastly Vision

Open Otherworld Portal

A rift opens in the mortal world that leads to the Otherworld. The portal stays open for an hour per Composure spent to cast the spell. The spell may also be used to open a portal in the Otherworld to the mortal world.

Difficulty: 6
Bleed Required: 3
Toll: 3
Casting Time: 1 day
Major Shock: Seeing the Great God Pan

Possession

Causes the caster to influence the mind of another human, allowing them to speak through their mouth and see through their eyes and act as they would act. The possessed are oblivious to their actions while influenced, waking up with no memory of their activities once the possession has ended. The caster must be able to see or know of the victim's location in order for the spell to work. The possessed will never harm themselves as doing so would do great psychological damage to the possessor. The spell effect lasts 1 hour per Composure spent.

Difficulty: 5
Bleed Required: 1
Toll: 2
Casting Time: 10 minutes
Major Shock: Corruption

Resurrection

The caster is able to bring a body back from the dead. By laying their hands on the corpse and uttering the recitation of resurrection, the caster feeds some of their life force into the body in order to ignite the spark of life once more. The body must have been dead for less than 24 hours for the spell to work.

Difficulty: 8

Bleed Required: 3

Toll: 4 (may only be deducted from Health)

Casting Time: 2 hours

Major Shock: Corruption

Séance

A group joins hands and invokes the spirits of a particular location. Once summoned, any spirits in the area will be able to communicate with the group through the lead caster, speaking in a strange guttural voice. During the séance, objects around the room may move or even be destroyed and participants will feel a queasiness well up in their stomachs as the realm of the dead joins the living. The séance spell must be undertaken by two or more people.

Difficulty: 5

Bleed Required: 1

Toll: 2

Casting Time: 10 minutes

Major Shock: Shaken

Speak with Great God

The spell allows the caster to converse with the Great God who resides in the Otherworld, usually using an obsidian scrying mirror. The caster may speak with the god for an hour after the spell is cast.

Difficulty: 5
Bleed Required: 2
Toll: 3
Casting Time: 1 hour
Major Shock: Dread

Spirit Seal

A magical seal is created on a threshold to prevent spirit beings from crossing. This usually requires the spreading of salt and the carving of wards on the threshold surface. The seal lasts for 1 day per Composure spent to cast the spell.

Difficulty: 4
Bleed Required: 1
Toll: 1
Casting Time: 10 minutes
Major Shock: Dread

Summon Great God Avatar

Calls forth the avatar form of a Great God from the Otherworld into the mortal world. The avatar appears within the spell's location, able to act on their own free will unless bound with a spell.

Difficulty: 8
Bleed Required: 3
Toll: 3
Casting Time: 3 hours
Major Shock: Corruption

Trap Soul

The victim's soul becomes ensnared within a mineral, such as a ruby or emerald. Their physical body becomes a vacant shell that can act independently but without emotion or drive, their eyes glassy and voice monotone. A vacant body is in danger of becoming a husk.

Difficulty: 5
Bleed Required: 2
Toll: 2
Casting Time: 1 hour
Major Shock: Time to Panic

Unbind Great God Avatar

This spell releases a bound avatar, removing any magical wards around it.

Difficulty: 6
Bleed Required: 3
Toll: 3
Casting Time: 1 hour
Major Shock: Shaken

Veil Sight

The caster can see the tendrils of Bleed erupting from the Veil like strands of golden hair in the breeze. If there is Bleed in the location the spell is cast, the caster knows its level.

Difficulty: 4
Bleed Required: 0
Toll: 1
Casting Time: 1 minute
Major Shock: Dread

CREATING WEIRD FOLK HORROR INVESTIGATIONS

There are strange things lost and forgotten in obscure corners of the newspaper.

Far Off Things

After playing through the mystery in this book, it's likely that you will feel the Otherworldly pull to craft your own investigations for your players. This is perfectly natural and indicative of a creative mind. Horror can be quite a tricky genre to write roleplaying investigations for, more so than fantasy adventures or cyberpunk heists. Horror relies heavily on mood, and Machen's stories have a certain mood to them that you will want to emulate. This section is designed to do just that: help you create a mystery specifically for *The Terror Beneath*.

HORROR VERSUS TERROR

While this book frequently uses the term horror for its genre, it's useful to determine what horror actually means and how it differs from terror. Horror itself is the reveal: looking upon the frightening thing and gasping with revulsion. Terror is the dread in the pit of your stomach before the true horror is revealed. Machen was a master of terror, using his investigators to put together each vile piece of the puzzle before the horror rears its head. As a reader you're slowly realising that things aren't quite right and as new clues are turned up the terror escalates, your palms begin to sweat and your pupils dilate. When running a game of *The Terror Beneath*, it's this reaction that you want to elicit from your players. It's these moments of heart-pounding apprehension that the players will talk about for years to come. When you're creating an investigation, come up with a list of 'terror points': elements of a mystery that cause that feeling of dread. It could be a dark staircase that leads into a basement where soft breathing can be heard, or maybe a forest whose trail leads by an abandoned shack whose windows flicker with a baleful green light.

METROPOLIS OR WILDERNESS?

One of the big decisions to make before you design an investigation is where you want to set it. The two settings in *The Terror Beneath*, the London Metropolis and the Welsh Wilderness evoke different sides of Machenesque horror and a unique 'feel' of investigation.

In a London Metropolis mystery, the plot will largely revolve around the Otherworld's incursion into civilisation and the corrupt people who stand to gain from this. Greedy aristocrats in secret societies continue their quest for unimaginable wealth, unearthing the dread secrets of the Great Gods to grant them their wish – but at what cost? Cruel politicians haunting Westminster in their bid to accumulate more power discover secret files of the Weird Office that hint at the means to conquer another world beyond our own. Warped scientists who wish to peer beyond the Veil use human experiments against their will, only to unmask the true face of fear. Investigators will find

themselves running around London on the trail of pagan evils hidden amongst the forgotten alleys and glittering monuments of the capital. Use the details in the London Metropolis section of this book to spark inspiration for your own investigations. Use well-known landmarks and twist them into something grotesque (even more effective if the players are familiar with the location – perhaps even having visited them before). There are also numerous secret societies with terrifying goals that can offer excellent hooks for your game. The internet is a great place to find out more about 1920s London.

A Welsh Wilderness mystery is designed to create a more traditional folk horror feel, where nature and the ancient things that crawl within the woods, hills and valleys are the major threat to the investigators. Away from the city, investigators will need to survive in a land where an overflow of Bleed

springs from ancient monuments, lost ruins and musty cairns, energies that are harnessed by witch cults and terrible beings thought lost to myth. Awful twig figures bound in string hang from tree branches creating a warning for curious trespassers. Villagers are seen prostrating themselves around a lake as something large ripples through the water. Miners return from the mountains unable to speak about the vile skittering things they saw in the dark. It should be clear to the players that this is no bucolic country walk, but an excursion into an old and terrible place that plainly wants them dead or worse. While Machen's stories can be used as inspiration for Welsh Wilderness mysteries, feel free to pull on other sources such as the tales of Algernon Blackwood or films like *The Ritual* or *In the Earth*.

Using Maps

Having a map of London can be handy to roll out on the table during a session to show where the investigators are and to help them plot their routes. Cassini Maps do a 1920 edition of the London city map that's accurate to the period, which adds authenticity and immersion. In my own games I've even used a Tiberius coin I bought from a well-known internet auctioning site to mark out where the players are at any point.

START AT THE END

One of the easiest ways to create a mystery is by starting with the final threat and working backwards. Begin by looking at the Dwellers in Twilight section to find something that catches your attention. For instance, a magus in a London Metropolis setting could be using the wine of Dionysus at a grand party in an attempt to summon the god.

The obvious climax of the investigation is having to prevent the party attendees from going mad from the wine and summoning the avatar of Dionysus. From this, you can start coming up with themes and ancillary characters: forbidden wine, bestial lunacy, decadence, bull heads, aristocrats, Bright Young Things. Perhaps the magus has already been testing the wine on inhabitants of a poorhouse causing people to riot and kill in broad daylight.

This offers you a good hook: a riot in an East End poorhouse leaves several dead and wounded. The offenders, overcome with bestial ravings, flee into the alleys, but leave behind a strange, empty wine bottle with a bull's head on the label. Another riot in another poorhouse puts the investigators face to face with one of the wine-drinkers, whose features have become beast-like. They trace the wine bottle to a supplier who happens to be a cultist of Dionysus, which in turn leads them to uncover the plot to create an environment of such rage that the magus can summon the god to offer them immortality from his cup.

Taking an example of the Welsh Wilderness setting, you might like the thought of using Arawn and the hounds of Annwn in a mystery based around the Wild Hunt of folklore. Every century a small village close to Newport is the scene of the Wild Hunt as Arawn sends his hounds to slay mortals and tear their souls from their lifeless bodies. Of course, the villagers all know the day is approaching that the Wild Hunt will begin once more, so they need souls to offer the Great God instead of their own. Rambling has quickly become a common past-time for city folk, so the villagers target an unfortunate hiking group to be their sacrifice to the hounds of Annwn and it's up to the investigators to save them before it's too late. As the hook, the Gold Tiberius Society is alerted to four hikers going missing near Newport and go to investigate, finding a disquieting community who keep antlered effigies in their barn and strange ceremonial garb stashed in the village hall.

DON'T OVERLOAD MYSTERIES WITH MONSTERS

Having too many types of terrifying beings in a mystery is a sure way to dilute the horror. Remember that creatures from beyond the Veil are rare and the people with the knowledge they exist are almost as uncommon. Consider having one true horror – the climactic source of terror (such as a Great God or Pan-born) and one 'helper' being (such as a group of voor or a cult). As the investigators move through each scene their exposure to these sources grow: first with a clue about the helper beings, then by seeing a helper being, and finally by revealing the true horror. Keep in mind that humans can be the most frightening part of a horror story, so don't get too hung up on trying to squeeze in too many ancient beings.

MAKE IT PERSONAL

Every PC has a Drive and a Terror Beneath that can provide you with excellent ways to up the personal stakes of a mystery. Tying these elements into your mystery or campaign can increase the players' immersion in the game and keep them invested. For example, taking the idea about the magus trying to throw a party to summon Dionysus, it makes sense for the Bright Young Thing investigator to receive an invitation to said party. Or with the example of the Wild Hunt, perhaps one of the investigator's Terror Beneath is having witnessed an antlered figure in the woods five years ago. Because each PC has a relationship with two investigators that they either rely on or protect, the stakes flow even wider than just the one character.

STRUCTURING SCENES

Once you have your premise, enemies and know how you're going to draw in your players through their Drives and motivations it's time to start structuring your investigation. Unlike some other games, GUMSHOE has a specific method of creating the elements of an investigation called **scenes**. There are several types of scenes you can use that each serve different purposes in your mystery. These scene types are as follows:

- An **Introduction scene** starts the story. It kicks off the case, presents the investigators with the question that must be answered and probably introduces a client. It also contains the elements of a Core scene.
- A **Core scene** provides enough information for the investigators to move onto another scene, and deeper into the central mystery, so long as they ask the right questions and looks in the right places.
- An **Alternate scene** presents a colourful, tense, diverting or otherwise entertaining scene, and perhaps some supplementary information, but need not be played out in order for the investigators to solve the central mystery. Alternate scenes may allow the investigators to skip some scenes designated as Core and still unravel the truth at the heart of the mystery.
- An **Antagonist Reaction** scene describes an event, usually bad, that unfolds in response to the investigators' actions. Its aftermath can provide

information, but doesn't have to. Most often, as the name implies, a villainous or obstructive character is taking action against the heroes. On occasion, the investigators might have to contend with impersonal or abstract forces, such as a storm.

- A **Conclusion scene** reveals the answer to the central question.
- The **Denouement** wraps up the story. It requires little or no prior writing from you, as its shape depends on events that happen during play. Usually, it features the investigators reporting back to the client and then a description of the case's grim coda, if any.

LEAD-INS

This entry lists other scenes that might precede this one when you play out the case.

• • •

LEAD-OUTS

This entry lists other scenes its core clues might lead the investigator to explore next. Think of Lead-Ins and Lead-Outs as bookmarks. When running the game, they orient you in relation to the other scenes. More crucially, when designing the mystery, they remind you to create options for the player. When every scene has only one Lead-In or Lead-Out, you've created a linear storyline that can only unfold in one way. When a scene can be reached, and followed up, in a number of ways, your player has meaningful choices to make. A few scenes with only one Lead-Out are fine, as the multiple Lead-Outs in other scenes allow investigators to pick up another thread of the investigation.

BODY TEXT

The body text of your adventure may consist of fully written material. For a mystery you're not planning to show anyone, point-form scrawlings will suffice. The more you write out, the less likely you are to miss a plot hole that might send you scrambling when you run the adventure. That said, the worst mystery is one you never run, because writing it all down feels too much like time-consuming homework.

Within a scene, deal with its basic elements in whatever order you prefer. Find a quick, evocative way to evoke the setting of each scene. Conjure a mood with details of location and, where applicable, background characters.

Describe the GMC around whom the scene revolves. Notes on their agenda enable you to decide what they do in response to an unexpected choice by the player. When writing compelling details into a supporting character's backstory, see to it that the player has some way of discovering or somehow interacting with that material. When you are caught up in the flow of adventure creation, this need can be surprisingly easy to forget.

Sometimes, to convey motivation, you have to include facts the witness would never intentionally reveal. Do so sparingly.

Avoid scenes that require the investigators to talk to more than one major character at a time. Portraying multiple supporting characters simultaneously as a GM will usually prove taxing for you and confusing for the player.

To include more than one GMC in a scene, break the scene up so that the investigator interacts with them in sequence, not simultaneously. Populate the scene with all the background extras you want. Shoot not for an empty world, but for a story where two-person dialogues predominate.

After setting out the context of the character and locale, segue into the clues the investigators seek in your scene. A bullet-point format for the clues, core and otherwise, enables you to find them quickly during play.

• • •

CLUE DELIVERY

You may find it helpful to arrange clues according to what the characters must do in order to discover them. Some are apparent: the investigators always notice them because they're out in the open, staring everyone in the face.

- Mr Kettering sweats and appears patently jittery.
- The contents of a wastebasket have been emptied on the desk.
- A body lies sprawled on the sofa, a bloody knife resting on its chest.

A cooperative witness will volunteer certain facts after the investigators introduces themselves and explains the basic nature of their enquiries. These may be honestly given, or they may be an effort to steer the investigators toward the witness' agenda.

Other clues are provided if asked: even a cooperative witness doesn't think of every relevant fact. To solve the case the investigators need merely to ask the right question.

Resistant clues require the use of an Investigative ability. In play you might ask the players to explicitly call them out, or you might just supply them when the players ask. You might also elect to provide them to a player who seems lost in the scene, on

the grounds that the character is a more experienced investigator than the player.

At any rate, whatever guidance you might find here becomes entirely provisional in the heat of play. The rhythm of information flow that the GM and players establish in the moment will always trump how you think things will go as you prepare.

• • •

CLUE TYPES

As previously mentioned, a Core scene must include at least one core clue – a clue that leads to another scene. Multiple core clues leading to different scenes give players choices to make, so include them where possible.

- A clue leading to an Alternate scene is an alternate clue.
- An Alternate scene might lead directly to no other scene. Or it might provide a secondary clue leading to a Core scene.
- Amid the clues, note possible Push benefits, if any. These non-informational benefits become available if the player agrees to pay a Push.
- Confine information available from Interpersonal abilities to those abilities the characters have.
- A pipe clue becomes significant only when combined with another piece of information gathered separately.
- A leveraged clue prompts a witness to spill his guts after being presented with another clue that the investigators uncovered earlier. It is usually accompanied by the use of an Interpersonal ability, such as Inspiration or Reassurance.

DWELLERS IN TWILIGHT

We have just begun to navigate a strange region; we must expect to encounter strange adventures, strange perils.

The Terror

As the mystical tendrils of the Otherworld leak into our fields, forests, suburbs and city streets, creatures unknown to science have begun to crawl up from the vast darkness beneath the world and long-dead gods lost to myth claw at the Veil. Meanwhile, the minds of men are twisted by the sweet seductive voices of these baleful presences, their compulsions turning to malice.

This section details a host of creatures, people and gods your players may come up against during a given session, collectively known as **beings**. It should be noted that these beings aren't overt in this world, nor are many part of a large population. The investigators may only ever come across one hounds of Annwn pack or a single dhol. Most of these beings should be used sparingly as not to desensitise the players to the many horrors you will throw at them across a campaign. Even creatures such as the voor, who exist in large writhing quantities, are hidden from humanity for the most part.

TYPES OF BEING

Each being is categorised into one of seven tags that determine their origin and nature.

• • •

GREAT GOD

These are beings of immense power, once worshipped by a vast population. But as time has moved on and their followers have dwindled, their sway over the mortal world has waned drastically. They are now relegated to their dwelling in the Otherworld where their machinations have turned to returning to our world and crushing civilisation as we know it. Most Great Gods have a domain, such as fertility, plague or war, along with a symbol to represent them. Should the investigators come up against a Great God in either its avatar or true forms, the best idea is to flee and figure out how to banish it back to the Otherworld. But maybe at that point it's already too late.

• • •

OTHERWORLD

Any being that primarily exists within the Otherworld has this tag. They rarely pass through the Veil without being summoned by someone in our world (largely by secret societies or mind-broken sorcerers). These beings tend to be formidable, able to ruin entire city streets in moments.

ANCIENT

Beings that have survived from prehistory are known as ancients. While they have an affinity with the Otherworld, some even able to cross the Veil with ease, they make their homes in the deep darkness of our world, whether in the bowels of a mountain or the shadows of a long-forgotten forest. While less powerful than beings of the Otherworld, ancients are often used as minions and spies for Great Gods or even mortal folk who have stumbled on their existence.

• • •

SPIRIT

These are also known as ghosts, spectres or wraiths. Spirits are the incorporeal echoes of the dead who continue to walk the earth as restless beings, often corrupted and malevolent. Some spirits can attach themselves to mortals to feed off their life force or control their actions, forcing them to act against their will.

• • •

CONSTRUCT

A being that is created through artificial means and brought to life through science, mysticism or a blend of the two are known as constructs. Most have no capacity to think for themselves, instead taking direct orders from a master. However, some have been known to become self-aware and turn against their master and human society as a whole as a result of their subjugation.

• • •

HUMAN

Native to our world, the human category broadly covers anyone who lives in our society. Humans are highly corruptible and capable of things even more heinous than the Great Gods.

• • •

BEAST

Covers any mundane animal, such as a dog, bird or spider. The further into the wilderness you get, the more dangerous beasts will appear.

READING THE STAT BLOCK

Numbers	How many individuals this being entry represents. A being might be a singular entity or a group of combatants. In the latter case, this may vary according to the number of PCs present. This changes the way you narrate the fight but requires no further numerical change to any of the being's numbers.
Difficulty	Name of Relative Challenge, followed by the Difficulty numbers for the Escape, Other and Kill goals.
Difficulty Adjustments	Conditions under which a bonus or penalty applies to the above Difficulties. A being might be, for example, harder to fight in the dark or easier to defeat when characters have researched its folklore or when choosing the Drive Away objective.
Toll	Number of points a character who made a Fighting test must spend to avoid taking a Minor Injury. Points may be spent from any combination of Athletics, Fighting and Health.
Tags	The category of being as detailed earlier in the section.
Injuries, Minor and Major	The Minor Injury card or Major Injury card inflicted by this being.

GAMEMASTERING BEINGS

The majority of non-human beings in *The Terror Beneath* are quite deadly in a straight fight, which makes it foolish for players to think they can take them on with brawn alone. The GM should consider what beings to include in their mystery, along with how many and where in the story they will be encountered. It's prudent to keep non-human beings to a minimum: familiarity is the enemy of terror. Focusing an investigation on one or two will suffice. This fits well with Machen's works where protagonists often uncover the sinister workings of a singular being (as in *The White Powder*), or where there are implied to be other creatures at play (*The*

Black Seal). Other antagonists can simply be mundane humans: hoodlums, gangsters, even police, who serve to get in the way and cause a few bruises, but nothing that the group can't overcome. Non-humans, though, usually require special knowledge to increase the investigators' chances of defeating them. Perhaps they need a certain book or to have a specific material such as fire.

Allow investigators to use their Investigative abilities such as Religion or Folklore to understand what they might be up against. Spending a Push will give them access to their Difficulty (try not to explain the numbers here – just the description will do in order to maintain immersion). Describe how they look: their teeth, claws or slithering appendages. How do they smell? What sort of noises do they make? Feel free to make these up where they're not noted in the stat blocks.

BEINGS

ADERYN Y CORPH (CORPSE BIRD)

Wretched things perch high in the shadowy trees of the Welsh wilderness. Wanderers have sometimes heard the shriek of a bird that has no name in scientific books. Occasionally they will sight a strange naked avian creature, wingless and with the husky skin of a corpse. In folklore this arboreal monster has come to be known as the aderyn y corph, whose cry is a portent of death.

Numbers	One per PC plus two
Difficulty	Weak (Escape 2, Other 3, Kill 3)
Difficulty Adjustments	-1 if the characters can't hear, +2 and Toll +1 if in an area of Bleed 2 or more.
Toll	0
Tags	Ancient
Injuries, Minor and Major	Beak Jabbed/Beak Stabbed

AFANC

The lakes of the Welsh wilds hide more than just weeds and fish. Unlucky fishermen and swimmers are on occasion dragged down to their dooms in the toothy grip of the afanc, a monstrous aquatic beast resembling the bastard child of a crocodile and beaver. These are impossibly fast swimmers, taking their prey in their jaws and plunging to the lake bed before devouring their quarry in a frenzied nightmare of gore. Even on land ramblers are seldom safe as the creature bursts from its murky home and runs madly towards its victims.

Numbers	One
Difficulty	Overwhelming (Escape 4, Other 7, Kill 8)
Difficulty Adjustments	-2 if the PCs sing the afanc's lullaby.
Toll	3
Tags	Ancient
Injuries, Minor and Major	Cough, Choke, Sputter/Lungful of Water

• • •

ARAWN

The King of the Underworld in Welsh mythology, Arawn's domain is the deep dark where even the shadows cast shadows. Folk in the wild hills are known to speak the phrase: 'Long is the day and long is the night, and long is the waiting of Arawn', for it is believed that once the spirit leaves the body it is hunted by his hounds and dragged through the Veil into the underworld.

Arawn is a figure cast in darkness, his face seldom seen from the gloaming that surrounds him. Only when sat upon his throne does he cast off this miserable shroud to reveal a rotten skull where a face should be, crooked antlers coated in flayed skin and pelt erupting from his cranium. His speech is darkness incarnate, more ancient than the stones and more powerful than the oceans.

The sockets of his eye blaze madly with a green flame like a will-o-wisp and with a stare that would shake time itself.

Numbers	One
Difficulty	Too Awful to Contemplate (Escape 5, Other 8, Kill 10)
Difficulty Adjustments	-1 if his hounds of Annwn have been destroyed, +2 if the Wild Hunt was successful.
Toll	4
Tags	Great God
Injuries, Minor and Major	Grazed/Puncture Wound

• • •

AUTOMATON

A machine built in the form of a human, forged in iron and brought to life by electricity. Automatons have great strength for all manner of uses and are usually built to only serve their creator. Some machinists weaponise their automatons to deal with their enemies, using their great iron arms to crush them into pulp.

Numbers	One
Difficulty	Superior (Escape 3, Other 4, Kill 6)
Difficulty Adjustments	-2 if submerged in water, +1 while in the presence of their master.
Toll	1
Tags	Construct
Injuries, Minor and Major	Automaton Strike/Crushing Automaton Strike

• • •

BLACK SERPENT OF THE CAIRN

Where the dead go, the serpent can be found. So goes the saying of those who eke out their living in the Black Mountains. A tale passed down through the generations, the black serpent is a gargantuan snake with fangs the size of swords and a tail that shimmers gold in the light. The creature burrows into the ground, erupting into cairns to devour the dead and grow even fatter. When bodies go missing from graveyards and the earth shakes like a quake, there are those who know the black serpent isn't far away.

Numbers	One
Difficulty	Superior (Escape 3, Other 4, Kill 6)
Difficulty Adjustments	+1 if it has been at least a day since last feeding, -2 if attacked with the lance of St George.
Toll	1
Tags	Ancient
Injuries, Minor and Major	Laceration/Restrained

• • •

CEFFYL DŴR (WATER HORSE)

Those who dwell in North Wales speak of a shapeshifter who comes to town in the form of a human with exaggerated equine features, smelling slightly of pond weed. The shapeshifter will charm the locals before bringing them into the wilderness, usually under the guise of a romantic liaison, before its form bulges and cracks into a horse-like beast with eyes like infernos. The ceffyl dŵr compels its quarry to mount it before riding into a murky lake, drowning its victim. Other times the creature flies high into the air before evaporating, letting the rider plummet to their demise.

Numbers	One per PC
Difficulty	Evenly Matched (Escape 3, Other 4, Kill 5)
Difficulty Adjustments	-1 if the character has read the folklore of ceffyl dŵr, +1 in an area of Bleed 1 or more.
Toll	1
Tags	Ancient
Injuries, Minor and Major	Contused/Crushed; or Cough, Choke, Sputter/Lungful of Water (if near a body of water)

CORPSE CANDLE

Prevalent in the Welsh marshlands and woods, corpse candles are fluttering balls of incandescent light that lure wanderers onto dangerous ground such as bogs or over ravines. Most wanderers believe the corpse candle is a campfire, but the more they try to reach the light the more the fire seems to recede into the night. Being close to this entity, one can feel the static in the air and a low rhythmic hum that triggers drowsiness in the victim. It isn't known whether corpse candles are the souls of those who were lured to their doom or malevolent spirits with their own agendas, but it's certain that laying eyes on one could be one's undoing.

Numbers	One
Difficulty	Tough but Outmatched (Escape 2, Other 3, Kill 4)
Difficulty Adjustments	+3 if the PCs are attempting to escape.
Toll	0
Tags	Spirit
Injuries, Minor and Major	Muzzy Headed/Heavily Sedated

• • •

CULTIST

A generic fanatical and dangerous cult member whose devotion to their leader and purpose borders on the suicidal. Any attempt to reason with a cultist usually ends badly, or even worse if you try to stop them from enacting their secret work.

Numbers	One per PC
Difficulty	Tough but Outmatched (Escape 2, Other 3, Kill 4)
Difficulty Adjustments	-1 if disguised as a fellow cult member, +1 in the presence of their leader.
Toll	0
Tags	Human
Injuries, Minor and Major	Cudgel Blow/A Thorough Thrashing

CYHYRAETH (FLESH WRAITH)

Drifting through the twilight air above lonely meandering rivers, one may be unfortunate enough to witness the beating leathery wings of the cyhyraeth. This ghoulish nightmare resembles a constantly out-of-focus spectre with long black fangs and flowing white hair. Its voice is a harsh whisper, speaking omens of doom upon those who gaze upon its foul glory.

Numbers	One
Difficulty	Superior (Escape 3, Other 4, Kill 6)
Difficulty Adjustments	+1 if a PC is suffering from an illness.
Toll	1
Tags	Spirit
Injuries, Minor and Major	Something in Your Eye/Puncture Wound

DHOL

Native to the Otherworld are the dhols, giant blind wormlike creatures who slither in the darkness underfoot, emerging only to feed on surface wanderers. With their beak-like mouths and rows of burnished copper scales, the dhol is the origin of every dragon tale in Great Britain, from the Lambton Worm to the Worm of Linton. But it is Wales where the dhol has been etched into the fabric of the nation, carrying its very image on their flag. Though rarely sighted, dhols do slip out of the Otherworld through their tangle of underground networks that cross the threshold between worlds. Usually these lead to caves, which is where the legends of dragons living in caves is thought to have originated.

Dhols come in many sizes, from the length of a village hall to the size of an entire street. The larger creatures are older than recorded time, and the most gargantuan of them all provided inspiration for the World Serpent in Scandinavian mythology.

Numbers	One
Difficulty	Vastly Superior (Escape 3, Other 6, Kill 7)
Difficulty Adjustments	-1 if a character is wielding a legendary weapon (i.e., Excalibur), +1 if in an area of Bleed 3.
Toll	2
Tags	Otherworld
Injuries, Minor and Major	Strong-Armed/Restrained

Ancient Dhol

Numbers	One
Difficulty	Overwhelming (Escape 4, Other 7, Kill 8)
Difficulty Adjustments	-2 if a character is wielding a legendary weapon (i.e., Excalibur), +1 if in an area of Bleed 2 or more.
Toll	3
Tags	Otherworld
Injuries, Minor and Major	It's a Miracle You're Alive/Massive Injuries

• • •

DIONYSUS

Hailing from the blasphemous vineyard of the Otherworld, Dionysus is the god of wine and ritualistic insanity. To his followers he offers ruby red wine to incite a frenzy of mad passion and fervour called the bakkheia. His true form is of a being enveloped in ivy, green tendrils reaching out and grasping a cup of exquisite wine said to immortalise those who would drink it. In his court his maenads, or 'the raving ones', dance eternally dressed in fresh bull hide. As an avatar, Dionysus appears often as a minotaur or centaur.

Avatar Form

Numbers	One
Difficulty	Overwhelming (Escape 4, Other 7, Kill 8)
Difficulty Adjustments	-2 if the PCs drank from his cup, +1 if surrounded by his maenads.
Toll	3
Tags	Great God
Injuries, Minor and Major	Cudgel Blow/Concussed

True Form

Numbers	One
Difficulty	Too Awful to Contemplate (Escape 5, Other 8, Kill 10)
Difficulty Adjustments	-2 if attacked with a thyrsus staff.
Toll	4
Tags	Great God
Injuries, Minor and Major	Picked up and Thrown Hard/Monstrous Battering

• • •

DOG

Use this profile for trained guard dogs or fierce feral dogs willing to attack humans.

Numbers	Two or three per PC
Difficulty	Weak (Escape 2, Other 3, Kill 3)
Difficulty Adjustments	-2 on a Natural History Push, +1 if the PC is trespassing.
Toll	0
Tags	Beast
Injuries, Minor and Major	Laceration/Bitten

DOPPELGANGER

One of the outcomes of a tryst between a mortal and a being of the Otherworld is a doppelganger. This strange, gangly offspring emerges into the world with an entirely featureless face, often resulting in the parent abandoning the creature in horror. But on this blank skin canvas the doppelganger can echo the facial features of other people, even slightly altering bone structure and weight to almost exactly emulate someone else. The only telltale sign is the eyes. Eyes are so complex that the doppelganger retains the deep black iris they were born with. As creatures of two worlds, doppelgangers can move between the Veil, though it takes until adulthood to realise their ability to do this. Still, throughout their life they hear the calling of the Great Gods in their heads and to those gods they show slavish obedience.

Numbers	One per PC
Difficulty	Evenly Matched (Escape 3, Other 4, Kill 5)
Difficulty Adjustments	+1 if the doppelganger takes the form of one of the PCs or one of their relatives.
Toll	1
Tags	Otherworld and Human
Injuries, Minor and Major	Stab Wound/Slashed Throat

GANGSTER

A member of London's many organised crime families. Gangsters are known for their brutal activities, whether it's fraud, extortion or murder. Often in league with corrupt police officers, bringing down a crime family is an almost impossible task.

Numbers	One per PC
Difficulty	Evenly Matched (Escape 3, Other 4, Kill 5)
Difficulty Adjustments	+1 if their boss is around.
Toll	1
Tags	Human
Injuries, Minor and Major	Grazed/Shot

• • •

GWYLLGI (CORPSE DOG)

Sighted in North Wales and on the Isle of Anglesey, the gwyllgi is an ancient creature that takes on the form of a fearsome black wolf three times the size of a normal wolf. Unlike a wolf, its face appears to have had its flesh flayed, revealing the bloody skull beneath and blazing red eyes in dark sockets. Those who have survived an encounter with the so-called corpse dog speak of the stench of rotten meat and the unholy cry, like that of a fox and a bear blended together. Wherever they go plant life is corrupted, rotting away within days of being in the creature's presence. Some hunt in packs, cornering their prey and surrounding them before the inevitable feast begins. Some magi have managed to tame the gwyllgi with potent magic and use them as watchdogs.

Numbers	One
Difficulty	Superior (Escape 3, Other 4, Kill 6)
Difficulty Adjustments	+1 if the moon is full, -1 if their magus owner is defeated, +1 Toll if in an area of Bleed 1 or more.
Toll	1
Tags	Ancient
Injuries, Minor and Major	Laceration/Flesh Wound

Gwyllgi Pack

Numbers	Four to six
Difficulty	Overwhelming (Escape 4, Other 7, Kill 8)
Difficulty Adjustments	+1 if the moon is full, -1 if their magus owner is defeated, +1 Toll if in an area of Bleed 1 or more.
Toll	3
Tags	Ancient
Injuries, Minor and Major	Laceration/Flesh Wound

• • •

GWYLLON (NIGHT WANDERER)

Taking the guise of an old lady, the gwyllon is a spirit who walks the night among the mountains, forests and lonely roads. In her mortal life she was a witch who dabbled in the blackest of sorcery. Those who witness the gwyllon are frozen to the spot as her hideous visage slowly floats towards them, a wicked grin crawling over her pale face. Often she leads wanderers astray, only to feast on them once they become weary. In folklore it's said that the gwyllon greatly fears iron, so travellers of old would always carry an iron knife or handful of nails with them should they run across the ghast.

Numbers	One
Difficulty	Superior (Escape 3, Other 4, Kill 6)
Difficulty Adjustments	-1 if any character is wielding a weapon forged of iron, +2 if in an area of Bleed 2 or more.
Toll	1
Tags	Spirit
Injuries, Minor and Major	Clawed/Eviscerated

HOODLUM

Full of fight and low on brains, these untrained brawlers infest decaying neighbourhoods.

Numbers	One per PC plus two
Difficulty	Weak (Escape 2, Other 3, Kill 3)
Difficulty Adjustments	+1 if characters are drunk.
Toll	0
Tags	Human
Injuries, Minor and Major	Black and Blue/Badly Beaten

• • •

HOUND OF ANNWN

In Welsh folklore, the hounds of Annwn were spectral dogs used by Arawn of the Otherworld during the Wild Hunt. Those living in the Welsh wilds believed that to hear the baying of one of these hounds would foretell a death. In reality these beasts barely resemble what you would call a dog at all. While they have four legs, the hounds of Annwn are translucent white, headless things the size of an adult wolf. They move at unnatural speeds, pouncing on their prey and letting out an eerie groaning sound that paralyses their victim. Then the stump of their 'neck' opens into a slavering maw, a large scarlet tongue lolling out, before devouring its quarry.

Hounds of Annwn are native to the Otherworld where they are bred by Nodens to hunt beings both within and out of the Otherworld.

Numbers	One
Difficulty	Evenly Matched (Escape 3, Other 4, Kill 5)
Difficulty Adjustments	+1 if it is Christmas, -2 if the characters have researched Nodens, if Bleed is 2 or more the margin to gain a Major Injury is reduced by 1.
Toll	1
Tags	Otherworld
Injuries, Minor and Major	Annwn Bite/Annwn Paralysis

Hounds of Annwn Pack

Numbers	One per PC
Difficulty	Superior (Escape 3, Other 4, Kill 6)
Difficulty Adjustments	+1 if it is Christmas, -2 if the characters have researched Nodens, +2 versus up to two characters.
Toll	1
Tags	Otherworld
Injuries, Minor and Major	Annwn Bite/Annwn Paralysis

• • •

HUSK

Sometimes, whether through the machinations of strange sciences or sinister occult rituals, the soul can depart from the body, leaving the space that remains open to becoming inhabited by dark, primordial forces transforming the victim into husks. People of the cloth have long since called these incidents 'demonic possession', but the beings that fester within these bodies are far older and more malevolent than anything conjured by hell. The husk may look just like the same person whose soul was banished, but their faces are often contorted into a foul visage and their movement erratic, as if the dark forces within are getting used to wearing their new flesh suit. Now having the ability to do physical harm in the realm of mortals, husks often turn to indiscriminate violence and murder, continuing until their body is put to rest or they are removed through science or incantation.

Numbers	One per PC
Difficulty	Evenly Matched (Escape 3, Other 4, Kill 5)
Difficulty Adjustments	+1 if encountered at an area of Bleed 1 or more.
Toll	1
Tags	Spirit
Injuries, Minor and Major	Badly Hurt/Draggy

JEELO

A jeelo is a spider-like being from the Otherworld that spins webs of lost memories in which to catch its prey. Its carapace is covered in glittering gemstones, each containing a wailing soul the jeelo has devoured. Using its memory silk, the jeelo can cross into the realm of human dreams where it may present itself in many forms. In some cases, the jeelo influences the human to fetch fresh new souls by having its new companion devour the hearts of their victims. Their soul transfers from the human vessel to the jeelo's web through dreaming, where the jewelled spider can finish off its prey. The jeelo's human vessel loses all memory of their murderous activities, as these memories are lost on the jeelo's web. The jeelo's soul gems are coveted by sorcerers, who can use them in their foul rituals or forge them into daggers that can be used to destroy dream-based beings.

Numbers	One
Difficulty	Vastly Superior (Escape 3, Other 6, Kill 7)
Difficulty Adjustments	-2 if a PC is wielding a dream-forged weapon, +1 if confronted in a dream.
Toll	2
Tags	Otherworld
Injuries, Minor and Major	Swallow Your Soul/You Are Mine

LLAMHIGYN Y DWR (WATER LEAPER)

Those who reside near lakes or swampland sometimes find their livestock gone or butchered by a mysterious entity. Some speak of a shadow seen leaping through the air followed by a tremendous rumbling croaking sound. Fishermen find their lines cut and their bait ruined, while those less fortunate are struck down by a vile poison that causes their flesh to rot away from their bones. Legends speak of the water leaper: a great frog-like being, bulbous of eye, with vast ragged wings like a bat's and a stinging tail that can strike in a flash. The water leaper is cunning, toying with humans as a cat would with a mouse, before striking. Farmers living close to a water leaper lair will make sacrifices, animal and human, to appease the beast below. Some communities have even turned to worship this vile creature as their idol, forcing sacrifices to drink of its poison in a ghastly rite.

Numbers	One
Difficulty	Overwhelming (Escape 4, Other 7, Kill 8)
Difficulty Adjustments	+1 if the PCs are in or on water, -1 if it witnesses its spawn being destroyed.
Toll	3
Tags	Ancient
Injuries, Minor and Major	Contused/Crushed

MAD SCIENTIST

'Mad scientist' is a catch-all term for anyone who uses science and technology to forward their own sinister agendas, often combining occult knowledge with scientific know-how to penetrate the secrets of the Otherworld. Some may be entirely lucid, believing what they are doing is for the progress of humankind after the nightmare of the Great War, while others have succumbed to the seduction of the Otherworld, serving one of the Great Gods.

Numbers	One
Difficulty	Tough but Outmatched (Escape 2, Other 2, Kill 4)
Difficulty Adjustments	-2 versus the entire cast of PCs.
Toll	0
Tags	Human
Injuries, Minor and Major	Blow to the Head/Ringing Cranium

• • •

MAENAD

A member of Dionysus' court, the maenad is the eternal dancer, wrapped in still-bleeding bull hide. Maenads are in a constant state of intoxication and frenzy brought upon by the maddening grapes of their god's vineyard. They each carry a thyrsus staff that they twirl and thrash with violent glee. Only depriving them of the mind-altering fruits they devour daily is enough to weaken a maenad.

Numbers	One per PC
Difficulty	Superior (Escape 3, Other 4, Kill 6)
Difficulty Adjustments	+1 if in the presence of Dionysus, -2 if deprived of grapes for a day.
Toll	1
Tags	Otherworld
Injuries, Minor and Major	Blow to the Head/Ringing Cranium

MAGUS

The magus exemplifies the pinnacle of the sorcerous craft, a person who has mastered dark books whose pages unlock the great mysteries of the world. While a magus typically comes from aristocratic stock, allowing them to pursue the magical arts at their leisure without the concern of working for a living, some practitioners sway far from the noble bloodline. It is said that you're as likely to find answers to the great mysteries in a stinking alley as you are in the warm confines of a library. These souls are often called 'gutter wizards' by the magical gentry, looked down on for their seemingly primitive practices. Nevertheless, all magi, no matter the origin, are interested in peeling back the Veil to discover the secrets beyond. Some make pacts with the Great Gods, agreeing to aid them in their agendas only for the promise of riches, power and even immortality (though rarely would a Great God follow through on their offer). Others seek to bind entities of the Otherworld into subservience, accessing points of tremendous Bleed to call forth their future minions.

Numbers	One
Difficulty	Superior (Escape 3, Other 4, Kill 6)
Difficulty Adjustments	+2 while in an area of Bleed 2 or more, -1 if they have no access to occult materials.
Toll	1
Tags	Human
Injuries, Minor and Major	Stab Wound/Slashed Throat

• • •

NODENS

Nodens is the Lord of Waters, a Great God who takes the form of a muscular but androgynous figure with stag-like horns jutting from his skull, draped in seaweed. While pleasant to behold, Nodens is wrathful like a storm in the ocean and as determined as a hunting pack. In the Otherworld, Nodens sits below the great sea in his vast palace with his nymph servants. Unable to move between worlds as an avatar, he sends out his beasts to patrol the rivers and seas of Earth, forever hunting in the murky depths. All the tales of sea and lake monsters throughout human history can be put down to Nodens' 'pets'.

Numbers	One
Difficulty	Too Awful to Contemplate (Escape 5, Other 8, Kill 10)
Difficulty Adjustments	+1 if fought within Nodens' domain, -1 if fought on land, +1 Toll if in an area of Bleed 3.
Toll	4
Tags	Great God
Injuries, Minor and Major	It's a Miracle You're Alive/Massive Injuries

• • •

NYMPH

Nymphs resemble beautiful men and women often bathing in pools or frolicking naked through the moonlit woods. Their sweet songs carry on the air, snagging the ears of a poor wanderer who can't help but investigate the origin of these honeyed melodies, finding nymphs swimming in pools or dancing in between the trees. They don't realise it, but the nymphs have enraptured the poor soul, rendering them utterly helpless while they are pulled down into the depths as a sacrifice to the gods. Each nymph is tied to a certain location, whether it's a waterfall, lake, tree or cave, and they don't venture far from their home.

Nodens' court is home to several nymphs of a more powerful variety who act as both servant and guardians of their god's domain.

Numbers	One per PC
Difficulty	Evenly Matched (Escape 3, Other 4, Kill 5)
Difficulty Adjustments	-2 if the PC's ears are covered, +2 if in Nodens' realm, Toll +1 if in an area of Bleed 2 or more.
Toll	1
Tags	Ancient
Injuries, Minor and Major	Strong-Armed/Restrained

• • •

PAN

Pan goes by many names: The Horned God, The Wild One, The Dread Faun, but all belong to the Great God who was once worshipped by some of the greatest civilisations in the world. While depictions of Pan show a goat-legged man with curled black horns frolicking in the woods, the entity has two forms: his true form and his avatar form, only the latter of which can successfully cross the Veil. While his avatar is more in-keeping with the aforementioned depictions, panpipes to his lips, his true form is one of true terror, an indescribable titan with dozens of crawling limbs and a thousand crimson eyes. His voice carries on the wind like the music of panpipes, understood only by his spawn. Pan can see into the minds of others, presenting himself as an idealised form before casting his foul spawn within them to be birthed weeks later. Looking upon Pan's true form is enough to send one into a spiral of madness. There have been several human victims of the god's dread will, including the girl Mary who would birth the pan-spawn Helen Vaughan, whose black-hearted malice saw her bring the London aristocracy to their knees. As with all Great Gods, Pan cannot die. If his avatar form is destroyed, he is once again banished back to the Otherworld. While it's theoretically possible to vanquish Pan in his true form, he will reform within months, more vengeful than ever.

Avatar Form

Numbers	One
Difficulty	Overwhelming (Escape 4, Other 7, Kill 8)
Difficulty Adjustments	-2 if Pan's pipes are destroyed, +1 if in an area of Bleed 3.
Toll	3
Tags	Great God
Injuries, Minor and Major	Laceration/Flesh Wound

True Form

Numbers	One
Difficulty	Too Awful to Contemplate (Escape 5, Other 8, Kill 10)
Difficulty Adjustments	None
Toll	4
Tags	Great God
Injuries, Minor and Major	It's a Miracle You're Alive/Massive Injuries

• • •

PAN-BORN

The offspring of Pan and a mortal is a vile and depraved being whose sole desire is to annihilate humanity. The child looks and acts like any other in its early years, but soon develops strange tendencies such as disappearing into the woods to talk with their 'imaginary' friends (though in reality this is often a conversation with an aspect of Pan himself). As they grow older, Pan-born show no empathy to their fellow humans, often relishing in the misery of others. At maturity their true purpose is revealed by Pan, whose delicate whispers in the heart of the forest order his offspring to bring

civilisation to its knees. The most famous Pan-born was Helen Vaughan who, like others of her nature, had the uncanny power to make others do her bidding. Through her seductive words several aristocrats were driven to suicide by hanging, and her reign of terror would have continued had she not been stopped by Villiers.

Though Pan-born look just like you or I, they are often described as having a serpent-like demeanour.

Numbers	One per PC
Difficulty	Superior (Escape 3, Other 4, Kill 6)
Difficulty Adjustments	-1 if the PCs know the true nature of the Pan-born, +2 if any PC currently has a Shock card.
Toll	1
Tags	Otherworld
Injuries, Minor and Major	Choked/Throttled

• • •

POLICE OFFICER

A uniformed 'bobby on the beat' wielding a truncheon. While police officers usually patrol alone, when there's trouble they will blow their whistle to call in reinforcements. The police generally approach supernatural claims with scepticism.

Numbers	One per PC
Difficulty	Evenly Matched (Escape 3, Other 4, Kill 5)
Difficulty Adjustments	+1 if any of the PCs are drunk and/or disorderly.
Toll	1
Tags	Human
Injuries, Minor and Major	Black and Blue/Badly Beaten

PRIMORDIAL OOZE

A drug synthesised with vinum sabbiti transforms humans into shapeless, slopping grey mounds of matter. The ooze will instinctively drip down into the dark places of the world, such as the London Underground or cellars, where it feeds off rats, pigeons and vagrants, engulfing them in its undulating gelatinous mass. The ooze can't think for itself, but can easily be controlled by those who cause it fear. Occasionally primordial oozes will join together to form a Mass Ooze.

Numbers	One per PC
Difficulty	Evenly Matched (Escape 3, Other 4, Kill 5)
Difficulty Adjustments	-1 if subject to fire.
Toll	1
Tags	Ancient
Injuries, Minor and Major	Strong-Armed/Enveloped

Mass Ooze

Numbers	One
Difficulty	Superior (Escape 3, Other 4, Kill 6)
Difficulty Adjustments	-1 if subject to fire.
Toll	1
Tags	Ancient
Injuries, Minor and Major	Strong-Armed/Enveloped

• • •

PROMETHEAN

Rather than view it as a warning, some black-hearted scientists saw Mary Shelley's Frankenstein as a guide to inspire them in creating new life from human remains. The result is the promethean – a chimera of human and sometimes animal parts stitched together and given the breath of life by scientific or mystical means. While decomposition has effectively stopped, prometheans still stink of rotten corpse, so their 'masters' often apply fragrances to their creation to mask the stench. These shambling beings have only a spark of intelligence for the most part, relying more on instinct and latent memory than actual logic. That said, some have been known to speak and think for themselves. It turns out these ones are far more dangerous than the others; after all, without intact nerve endings they tend to put up more of a fight than a normal human.

Numbers	One
Difficulty	Superior (Escape 3, Other 4, Kill 6)
Difficulty Adjustments	-1 if attacked with fire, -2 if attempting to reason with the creature, +1 if the creature is angered.
Toll	1
Tags	Construct
Injuries, Minor and Major	You Should See the Other Fellow/ Concussed

• • •

PWCA

In the deepest parts of rural Wales tales tell of beings who can change their shape into dogs, foxes, wolves and goats. These are the pwca, vile stunted creatures whose hunched form is voorish in nature but their wide golden eyes and slithering crimson tongues identify them as their own strange race. While the voor wallow in the deep dark, the pwca prefer to make their dens in tangled woodland, usually near a stream or pool where they can easily drown their victims. Some venture into nearby settlements in their animal form, only to spring on their quarry unawares and bleed them dry. Farmers are wary of the pwca around the festival of Samhain, scattering cold iron rods around their crops to keep the beasts at bay, lest their harvest become blighted.

Numbers	One per PC
Difficulty	Tough but Outmatched (Escape 2, Other 3, Kill 4)
Difficulty Adjustments	-1 if the PCs are carrying cold iron, +1 if faced in darkness.
Toll	0
Tags	Ancient
Injuries, Minor and Major	Jarred/Broken Bone

• • •

SIN EATER

As the dying lay on their bed, the cords of mortality snapping around them, so a sin eater crosses the threshold and takes a seat by the poor wretch. From a bag they produce tender raw meat, staring deep into the soul of the dying while chewing mouthfuls of bloody carcass and drowning it with beer. In moments the ritual is complete and the bed is devoid of life. The sin eater has offered absolution to the deceased by devouring their sins, corrupting their soul even further. With a belly full of temptation, gluttony and malice the sin eater departs to carry out the very evils they have absorbed.

Numbers	One
Difficulty	Evenly Matched (Escape 3, Other 4, Kill 5)
Difficulty Adjustments	+1 for each Shock card the PCs have.
Toll	1
Tags	Human
Injuries, Minor and Major	Cudgel Blow/A Thorough Thrashing

• • •

SOLDIER, CORRUPTED

Those who have braved the front lines have seen the worst that humanity has to offer. The survivors of the Great War returned shell-shocked and fragile. Unfortunately, this disposition left some open to the foul whispers of the Otherworld, bending them to the will of the Great Gods and becoming soldiers on the front between the Veil and civilisation.

Numbers	One per PC
Difficulty	Evenly Matched (Escape 3, Other 4, Kill 5)
Difficulty Adjustments	+1 if the PC is surprised by the attack.
Toll	1
Tags	Human
Injuries, Minor and Major	Grazed/Shot

• • •

TWRCH TRWYTH (GREAT BOAR)

The Twrch Trwyth is a monstrous boar who was said to have done battle with King Arthur himself, having survived all these centuries in an undetermined Welsh forest. The great boar is essentially a god himself – almost invincible and capable of such destruction that even Arawn might look away. The size of a house, with two yellowing tusks coated in gore and two beady yellow eyes that see perfectly in the dark, the Twrch Trwyth is a being whose very image drives people to madness. But as with many beings of the elder days, the great boar has its devotees who seek to bring about the destruction of all civilisation by waking the beast and causing it to rampage.

Numbers	One
Difficulty	Too Awful to Contemplate (Escape 5, Other 8, Kill 10)
Difficulty Adjustments	-2 if attacked with Excalibur.
Toll	4
Tags	Ancient
Injuries, Minor and Major	Picked up and Thrown Hard/ Monstrous Battering

VENUS

Has there ever been something so beautiful and wretched as the goddess Venus? She is the embodiment of seduction and manipulation, a being whose powers can sway the minds of anyone she wishes. While the classical depiction of Venus stays true to her avatar form as a woman of beauty beyond measure, her true form is an ever-shifting mass of legs, arms and heads surrounded by an intoxicating perfume that triggers desire in the hearts of those who smell it.

Avatar Form

Numbers	One
Difficulty	Overwhelming (Escape 4, Other 7, Kill 8)
Difficulty Adjustments	-2 if the PCs have destroyed the shrine of Venus, +1 if any of the PCs drank from Hadrian's Well, +1 if in an area of Bleed 3.
Toll	3
Tags	Great God
Injuries, Minor and Major	Distracted/Slashed Throat

True Form

Numbers	One
Difficulty	Too Awful to Contemplate (Escape 5, Other 8, Kill 10)
Difficulty Adjustments	-2 if unable to smell her intoxicating perfume.
Toll	4
Tags	Great God
Injuries, Minor and Major	Through the Ringer/Breaking Point

VOOR

Throughout time the voor have gone by many names: the fair folk, the little people, tylwyth teg, fairies. Tales tell of beings haunting long barrows, dark forests and misty hills, a prehistoric civilisation of squat, terrible beings whose very nature is to kidnap, devour and breed. Victorian folklorists ameliorated these beings into fantastical winged cherubs who delighted children upon their discovery, usually in a merry ring of toadstools. But the truth of the voor is far more terrible and a world away from the cheery image conjured by children's writers at the time.

The voor existed before humanity set foot into the world. Those who have encountered one of these vile creatures describe their squat body, standing no more than four feet tall, with leathery skin and dark, almond-shaped eyes. Their yellowed teeth are jagged, useful for tearing into the flesh of their captives. The air around them reeks of decay; so potent is this stench that when a group of voor are together the odour is overwhelming.

They make their lairs in the deep gloom of the world, creating wretched colonies that sometimes travel for miles within underground tunnels, springing out into the countryside or, very occasionally, into civilisation. These labyrinths are of unknown size and complexity, but some scholars believe that a large group of voor lives within the Welsh countryside and their lairs stretch all the way to London. There have been several sightings of small, hairy prehistoric beings in the shadows of London's poorest streets. Sometimes a homeless person is dragged into the dark sewers below, while other times bodies wash up on the shores of the River Thames, their flesh carved with strange symbols.

The voor's guttural and monosyllabic language is known as 'black speech', while their scratched symbols of whorls and runes are sometimes referred to as 'Aklo script'. Aklo covers most voorish structures, such as megaliths raised in the hazy mists of time, carved using Stone Age flint tools.

During their festivals they seek sacrifices in the outside world, ambushing travellers, villagers and even city folk, dragging them into the belly of their dim world where blasphemous dances and awful chants prelude a sacrifice.

The voor are able to travel between the Otherworld and our world using voorish structures such as pyramids and monoliths.

Numbers	One per PC plus three
Difficulty	Evenly Matched (Escape 3, Other 4, Kill 5)
Difficulty Adjustments	+1 if in their subterranean lair, -1 if any character is carrying an open flame, while Bleed is 2 or more Toll increases by 1.
Toll	1
Tags	Ancient
Injuries, Minor and Major	Laceration/Flesh Wound

WITCH

From moon-haunted woods to damp London cellars, witches gather in foul cults to enact the blackest of magics with blood sacrifice and the drinking of the vinum sabbiti. Unlike the aristocratic magus who longs for the universe's secrets, the witch works with the powers inherent in the Otherworld to curse their enemies and bring about the end of the world. Witches hide in plain sight. They could be the sultry blonde caressing a martini glass in an affluent bar, a live-in nurse whose employers are oblivious of her midnight practices or a rural hermit who cackles at the moon knowing truths others dismiss.

Numbers	One per PC
Difficulty	Evenly Matched (Escape 3, Other 4, Kill 5)
Difficulty Adjustments	+1 after drinking the vinum sabbiti, +1 in an area of Bleed 2 or more.
Toll	1
Tags	Human
Injuries, Minor and Major	Witch Mark/Hexed

MYSTERY: DON'T SLEEP

There upon the floor was a dark and putrid mass, seething with corruption and hideous rottenness, neither liquid nor solid, but melting and changing before our eyes, and bubbling with unctuous oily bubbles like boiling pitch.

The Novel of the White Powder

This section contains a mystery for you to run with your group using the rules in this book. Before a session, you should make sure you read through and understand the main points of the mystery: the characters, locations and clue types within. You players won't always do what you think (in fact, they rarely do) so prepare to improvise a little to bring them naturally back on track. They might even have a great way to use an ability that isn't noted in the text, in which case you should roll with it and offer them a clue as a reward for their creativity.

In this mystery, a series of disappearances leads to the PCs uncovering a military sleep experiment whose subjects are slowly becoming tunnel-dwelling primordial beings with a large appetite.

• • •

THE HOOK

Ambrose informs the PCs of a disappearance two weeks ago: a dockworker who seemingly vanished into thin air.

• • •

THE VEILED TRUTH

The dockworker, Wilfred Abbott, was one of three soldiers drafted into a 1917 experiment conducted by Dr Robert Leyland to remove a human's need to sleep. As conventional methods were getting him nowhere, Dr

Leyland sought out an answer from an ancient sorcerous text called the Caerleon Tablet, which gave the ingredients for a potent concoction that would keep warriors awake for months at a time, sometimes years. He swore his staff to secrecy before conducting the rite. The experiment was considered a success by the military and the soldiers were brought into Operation *Moonwatch*, using their newfound capacity for sabotage and espionage. *Moonwatch* was totally off the official record and while the soldiers succeeded in their missions, they received no recognition for their bravery and were forced to return to civilian life.

Now, four years later, Abbott had started to become irritable, even violent. As a side effect of the ritual his body and soul eventually corrupted, melting into a primordial ooze and draining into the sewers. Now it prowls beneath the streets, seeking sustenance as the remaining soldiers begin to transform. As the ooze collects more soldiers its hunger grows and soon travellers of the London Underground will be in imminent danger.

• • •

ANTAGONIST REACTIONS

The primordial ooze spends most of the mystery feeding on rats down in the sewers. However, it eventually breaks out through a wall and makes it onto the London

Underground where it will devour an entire carriage of people before melting back into the hole to grow further.

SCENES

ROYAL ALBERT DOCK

Scene Type: Introduction
Lead-Outs: Walter Bigson, Silvertown

To start the mystery the investigators will be gathered by Ambrose in the Society offices at Red Lion Square. He passes them a newspaper whose headline reads of a docker's disappearance in unusual circumstances. According to the article, Wilfred Abbott hasn't been seen in a week after seemingly vanishing from Royal Albert Dock where he was employed by Waterson's Stevedores. Ambrose believes the police have all but given up on the mystery, putting it down to another dock-based fatality, likely falling overboard and drowning, but Ambrose is less convinced. The short article gives very little information, so he believes it prudent that the investigators pay a visit to Royal Albert Dock, East London.

When the investigators reach Royal Albert Dock, they see hulking vessels: merchant steamers tended to by swarms of dockers and one Atlantic transport liner called The Blue Sapphire being boarded by travellers to the United States. The dock is clotted by a complex of buildings, mostly shipping companies. Waterson's Stevedores is one of the less assuming structures hidden away behind a field of barrels. Inside is Harry Waterson, a wide-girthed man sporting a thick hedge of a moustache. His writing desk is littered with papers and manifests as he furiously scribbles down notes.

Waterson has little patience – he's a busy (and wealthy) man and believes he's told the police enough. Investigators can get him to open up a bit with:

- **Charm** (smooth-talk him with compliments, particularly about his self-made business).
- **Reassurance** (explain that they are trying to do what the police have failed to in finding out what happened to Abbott).

Waterson explains the following once he's more inclined to talk:

- Wilfred Abbott had been with the company for a year. He was a good worker, strong and seemingly never tired. He would sometimes put in day and night shifts. Some of the men thought him odd based on this fact.
- He had been showing some strange behaviour recently. He was generally quiet and kept to himself, but of late he was irritable and even struck one of the dockers, Walter Bigson, after an argument (Core scene: Walter Bigson).
- He was loading a Canadian steamer when he vanished. The vessel has since left port, but he got into a fist fight with one of the other dockers, Walter Bigson, before he vanished.
- His wife Mavis is understandably distraught. Their home is 23 Rose Terrace in Silvertown. Waterson had paid a visit two days ago to see how she was doing, but she barely spoke (Core scene: Silvertown).

• • •

WALTER BIGSON

Scene Type: Core
Lead-In: Royal Albert Dock
Lead-Outs: Cecil Graves, Greenwich Metal Works, Silvertown

Walter is a skinny man with weasel-like features and a whopping black eye. He is helping unload an Indian ivory ship, barking at two other dockers in a cutting East End accent. Asking specific questions nets the following answers:

- He didn't see eye to eye with Wilfred, but he would never start a fight with him. They were both loading up the Canadian steamer's hold when out of nowhere Wilfred threw a swing at him. His eyes burned with rage and it looked like he'd spilled some oil on himself.
- He tried to calm Wilfred in his rage, but Wilfred just continued to punch him. **Assess Honesty** reveals this to be false and in response Walter will admit that he gave him a few belts on the chin for good measure.
- Walter turned away for a split second after being punched and Wilfred was gone. There was no way he could have got out without him noticing as there was only a single exit. He just vanished. There were dozens of dockers around outside the cargo hold too who would have seen him.
- Wilfred had been getting more erratic over the last few weeks. Walter had seen him out a few nights at The Jive House

with a fellow who never seemed to remove his military uniform (Core scene: Cecil Graves) and a chap called Barney Robbins who a mutual friend works with over at the metalworks (Alternate scene: Greenwich Metal Works).
- Wilfred's wife has visited several times since his disappearance to no avail. The police have all but given up at this point so she's getting desperate (Core scene: Silvertown).

• • •

SILVERTOWN
Scene Type: Core
Lead-Ins: Royal Albert Dock, Walter Bigson
Lead-Outs: Greenwich Metal Works, Cecil Graves, Dr John Bowbridge

Arriving at Wilfred's residence in Silvertown, Mavis answers the door: a dark-skinned woman with a mass of curly black hair and infinitely sad eyes. **Reassurance** or **Negotiation** will help get the investigators

in the house to interview her. She delicately lights up a cigarette and slumps back in a worn chair by the fire. A malnourished tabby cat hops up and nuzzles into her lap. A British army uniform is laid out pristinely on the chair opposite.

She tells them she's spoken with the police several times but they have yet to find out where Wilfred went, and she believes they've lost interest.

- The uniform is Wilfred's. He served in the Great War in the City of London Rifles but never spoke about it with her.
- He's a caring man, but over the past couple of months his behaviour grew strange. He would be prone to sudden outbursts, shouting and pounding his fists on the walls. He smashed a mirror, which hasn't been cleaned up. **Notice** will reveal the mirror shards have a slight black residue on them, mixed with dried blood. The residue has a pungent odour. **Chemistry** shows this isn't oil or paint, but possibly organic.
- He was taking medication for his insomnia, but it didn't seem to be working. **Notice** reveals the pill bottle on a shelf, with the name Dr John Bowbridge scrawled on the label (Core scene: Dr John Bowbridge).
- He would never sleep, always having red rings around his eyes.
- **Military History** will show the rank depicted on the uniform to be a lieutenant, but also a red triangular badge that fits no official rank. Mavis doesn't know what this is.
- When he wasn't working, he would spend his time in Soho at The Jive House with his friend Cecil Graves. **Culture** reveals The Jive House to be a popular haunt for ex-soldiers on account of the owner being a former captain of the Royal Fusiliers (Core scene: Cecil Graves).
- Before he went missing, he was talking about going to visit Barney Robbins

who served with him. He works at the Greenwich Metal Works as a riveter (Alternate scene: Greenwich Metal Works).

If the investigators take a look around the small house, **Notice** will uncover a writing desk with strange jagged symbols carved into it. **Linguistics** show these to be a language unlike anything seen, potentially one that's been invented. **Archaeology** reveals that there have been tablets found with similar symbols that were on show at the British Museum two years ago (Alternate scene: British Museum).

• • •

CECIL GRAVES

Scene Type: Core
Lead-Ins: Walter Bigson, Silvertown
Lead-Outs: Greenwich Metal Works, Dr John Bowbridge, Experiment Basement

The investigators will find Cecil Graves pouring whisky down his gullet at the bar of The Jive House, where a group of jazz musicians are playing a slow, disjointed number while a woman in a long dress and feather boa croons softly into the microphone. Graves is easy to find on the account of his full uniform and tag reading Second Lieutenant Graves. **Notice** or **Military History** reveals he has the same red triangle insignia as Wilfred. Sweat drips from his brow and his hand visibly shakes as he puts down his glass and orders another from the concerned-looking waitress. Cecil is a young man with close-cropped hair and piercing blue eyes. Red rings circle his eyes and he smells slightly of rotten eggs. He answers questions while slugging back whisky:

- He doesn't know where Wilfred is. He last saw him the day before his disappearance.
- He hasn't slept in over a year and seems to only sleep once per year. **Biology** indicates this shouldn't be possible without the affected individual dying from exhaustion.

- Wilfred was talking about his 'last days coming up' and saying that 'he feels himself drawn to the underworld'.
- Cecil is reluctant to talk about the red triangle insignia but **Negotiation**, **Charm** or **Reassurance** will get him to whisper of a secret operation in 1917 called Operation *Moonwatch*.
- Operation *Moonwatch* was a covert initiative in the war where Cecil, Wilfred and Barney Robbins were subjected to an experiment that meant they rarely had to sleep, making them excellent spies.
- He doesn't remember much about the experiments themselves, but he mentions they were in a building on the south bank of the River Thames with a triangle on the iron gates and two gargoyles leering over. He remembers descending into the dark. **Dérive** reveals this to be located near Lambeth Bridge, and **Society** shows it to have been a temporary government building that was closed down after the war (Core scene: Experiment Basement).
- He saw Barney Robbins two weeks ago, the other soldier who was part of the experiment. He works at a sheet metal factory in Greenwich Metal Works. He didn't seem well and was saying similar things to Abbott (Alternate scene: Greenwich Metal Works).
- Cecil has been getting pills from Dr John Bowbridge in Belgravia, who Barney has also been seeing, but nothing seems to be helping. **Society** reveals Bowbridge to be a world-renowned specialist in sleep disorders (Core scene: Dr John Bowbridge).
- He becomes more erratic as the interview goes on, eventually shattering a glass on the ground and leaving abruptly.

Two hours after this scene, while stumbling home through London's back alleys, Cecil's body structure melts down into a black substance as he becomes a primordial ooze, sinking through the gutter to the sewers to meet with Wilfred (or the ooze that used to be Wilfred).

• • •

GREENWICH METAL WORKS

Scene Type: Alternate
Lead-Ins: Cecil Graves, Silvertown, Walter Bigson
Lead-Outs: Cecil Graves, Bowbridge

The glowing sparks of industry fill the cacophonous air as the investigators enter the metal works. As they explore, they hear shouting as Barney Robbins screams at one of the other workers. The words make little sense, sounding like a nonsense language. **Linguistics** reveals it sounds something akin to an ancient version of Brythonic Welsh, making out only certain words like 'we are the watchers' and 'underworld'. He is a young man with a long scar down his cheek and red rings around his eyes. He throws a punch at the other man and picks up a rivet gun, placing it against the man's head as he cries out in terror. The area reeks of rotten eggs. Due to the stress, investigators must succeed a Difficulty 4 **Composure** test or take a Cause for Concern/Time to Panic Shock card.

If the investigators try to intervene Barney is treated as a Corrupted Soldier (p.103), attacking them while roaring the same strange words. He has a -1 Difficulty if attacked with fire or equipment that would create a flame (i.e., welding equipment). Also allow them to test Difficulty 4 **Sneaking** to wrench the rivet gun from his hand, giving him a -1 Difficulty in combat.

If they decide against intervening, Barney will fire a rivet into the man's temple, killing him instantly. Investigators who see this must succeed a Difficulty 4 **Composure** test or take a The Shudders/Shaken Shock card.

If he kills his co-worker or defeats the investigators, he flees the scene, weaving between the machinery before collapsing into a primordial ooze down a grate. Even if the investigators make chase, they won't see the actual transformation but they will find thick black residue over the grate that leads to the waters below.

Should Barney die, his body collapses into a primordial ooze that slowly drips through the grated floor. This is going to be a strange and terrifying sight to the investigators who must succeed a Difficulty 4 **Composure** test or take a There's Something About Them/True Form Shock card.

Inspecting the black residue left by the ooze with **Chemistry** reveals it to be the same substance as was on Wilfred's mirror.

If the man he attacked is still alive, he's badly shaken and concussed. Other workers carry him away while they wait for an ambulance. The factory foreman, Lester Smith, comes to check on the investigators, his glasses steamed up from the heat of the factory floor. If they ask about Barney, Lester says the following:

- Barney works as a riveter, but over the past month it seems he's been afraid of using his gear.
- He had been visiting a sleep specialist in Belgravia (Core scene: Dr John Bowbridge).
- He has become increasingly short tempered over the last few weeks, lashing out at his fellow workers and becoming ever more insular.
- He knows Barney hasn't been sleeping on the count of the red rings around his eyes. Apparently when not working he whiles away the night at The Jive House with a military friend (Core scene: Cecil Graves).

• • •

EXPERIMENT BASEMENT

Scene Type: Core
Bleed: 1
Lead-Ins: Cecil Graves, Dr John Bowbridge
Lead-Outs: Dr Leyland, Pan's Grove, British Museum

The building is protected by a large iron gate sporting a large red triangle. The gate is chained and padlocked, while the rest of the building is surrounded by a high wall. A Difficulty 3 **Athletics** test will allow the walls or gate to be scaled, or the chains can be cut with professional chain cutters. Anyone failing scaling the walls will manage to climb over, but will stumble, reducing their **Health** or **Athletics** by 1.

Once in the grounds, the door to the building can be smashed open with a Difficulty 3 **Athletics** test.

The basement is a wide concrete room with several beds set up in the centre flanked by dusty oxygen tanks. Jars of ointments and salves line shelves, and filing cabinets are stuffed with medical paperwork. **Research** or **Notice** reveals several documents of note labelled 'Classified'. There are files on Wilfred Abbott, Barney Robbins and Cecil Graves, with their dates of birth and medical information listed. The paperwork goes into the results of several months of testing, how each is reacting to certain medication in an effort to stop them from requiring sleep. Each document is signed by Dr Alan Leyland of King's College London (Core scene: Dr Leyland).

Inspecting the jars, **Chemistry** reveals some labelled as acetylcholine, which is the chemical secreted by the hypothalamus that keeps humans awake. But one jar reads 'V.S.', containing a black, viscous liquid. **Occult** will reveal this to be vinum sabbiti, or witch's wine, said to be imbibed by practitioners of the dark arts to gain great abilities from their gods.

Notice will find a journal written by Dr Leyland outlining the progress he and his assistants from the university were making in 1917 for Operation *Moonwatch*. He mentions trial after trial and failure after failure with conventional medicine. He goes on to talk about getting help from one Mary Whitstable when things became desperate. Whitstable used a tablet with an unknown language to concoct a solution while reciting an incantation. While Leyland was sceptical of her methods, he couldn't deny that the potion worked.

A small stone tablet stands out among the documents, covered in strange writing that matches that found on Wilfred's desk. **Archaeology** reveals the stone and text to be similar to that found on the Seventy Stone displayed at the British Museum (Alternate scene: British Museum). The stone itself is a red colour, with **Geology** revealing this to be Old Red Sandstone.

Dérive or **Occult** can be used to know that Mary owns an occult bookshop in Leicester Square called Pan's Grove (Core scene: Pan's Grove).

$$\bullet \ \bullet \ \bullet$$

DR LEYLAND

Scene Type: Core
Lead-Ins: Experiment Basement, Dr John Bowbridge
Lead-Outs: Dr John Bowbridge

A trip to Strand takes the investigators to King's College where quick inquiries point them in the direction of Dr Leyland who is currently in his office. He's an older man with wild grey hair and a nervous stutter. He will be closed up regarding questions about Operation *Moonwatch* unless the investigators have undeniable evidence to prove he was involved. In which case:

- He regrets his involvement, even after Operation *Moonwatch* was so successful in the eyes of his superiors.
- He has been monitoring his 'subjects' at a distance through Dr John Bowbridge, who has fed him information about their medical status (Core scene: Dr John Bowbridge).
- He believes that the vinum sabbiti ritual has set off a chain reaction in their DNA that eventually breaks down into the constituent building blocks of life. However, he doesn't know how long this process takes.

Dr Leyland will draw out a sample of black ooze from a refrigerator and place it under a microscope. Investigators peering into the microscope will see thousands of tiny blobs and lozenges writhing on the petri dish. **Geology** or **Natural History** will reveal these to be microbes that existed at the dawn of time, which eventually evolved into more complex life. Dr Leyland believes that the black ooze is an embodiment of the so-called 'primordial soup' that all life eventually emerged from billions of years ago. He's noticed that the thing has an aversion to fire, lighting a candle and showing the thing shrink away from the flame.

Suddenly the ooze leaps up and enters Dr Leyland's throat. As he falls to the ground, choking, the ooze begins to grow and engulf his body. Each PC must succeed a Difficulty 4 **Composure** test or take a The Shudders/ Shaken Shock card.

Quick-thinking investigators can try to burn the ooze away from his body, requiring a Difficulty 5 **Athletics** test to grab a nearby Bunsen burner. If the test succeeds the ooze retreats into the nearest grate, slopping into the sewers. Failure sees Leyland completely enveloped in the ooze after which he raises up and attempts to escape down the grate. If the investigators try to stop the creature, a fight initiates with the primordial ooze (p.102).

• • •

DR JOHN BOWBRIDGE

Scene Type: Core
Lead-Ins: Cecil Graves, Silvertown, Dr Leyland
Lead-Outs: Dr Leyland, Experiment Basement

A soft-spoken man in his late 50s, Bowbridge is welcoming of the investigators into his cramped doctor's offices in Belgravia. If pressed about Barney, Cecil or Wilfred's medication he states that he can't break doctor–patient confidentiality, though **Reassurance** or **Negotiation** will get him to reluctantly open up, or if they mention that his patients' lives could be in danger.

He notes that all have been patients with him for a number of years, but it's only within the past few weeks that they had been displaying strange and erratic behaviour. Bowbridge believes that the men are experiencing so-called 'shell shock'. Barney told him of his recurring dreams of being within the earth and moving through it, as if he were melting into the very crust of the world into a domain of true darkness where a dreadful horned figure would sit on a great throne. **Occult** or **Folklore** reveals this could be a description of Arawn, the god of the underworld.

Bowbridge declines to mention that he has been sending samples of their sweat and saliva to Dr Leyland at King's College in order for him to assess the black discharge they seem to be secreting. **Notice** to see a file with Dr Leyland's name on, containing some notes on the above (Core scene: Dr Leyland). If pressed with **Reassurance**, **Negotiation** or **Charm**, he explains that Leyland had asked him to keep an eye on these three patients in particular. During the war Bowbridge worked with Leyland on Operation *Moonwatch*, based in a now-defunct government building close to Lambeth Bridge, which can be identified with **Dérive** (Core scene: Experiment Basement).

• • •

BRITISH MUSEUM

Scene Type: Alternate
Lead-Ins: Cecil Graves, Silvertown, Dr Leyland
Lead-Outs: Experiment Basement

Entering the vast British Museum the PCs meet with Catherine Wheeler, the Curator of Ancient Civilisations at the museum. She speaks giddily of all matters pertaining to her expertise, especially when the subject of Aklo texts comes up. Any of the PCs with some historical credibility, such as a curator or archaeologist, will be able to secure some of Catherine's time to talk about the Aklo tablet that was on display up until recently, now kept in storage for study.

She explains that the tablet they have in their care is from a dig in the Black Mountains of Wales where archaeologists were looking for evidence of an ancient civilisation who once lived there. The stone, crafted from Old Red Sandstone, they dubbed the 'Seventy Stone' for its 70 strange characters carved into the surface. Anyone with **Linguistics** can see that these symbols are not of any script known to antiquity, and those with **Archaeology** note that the stone must be Neolithic – a time when writing didn't exist in that locality. Catherine is impressed with any of these assertions and agrees, almost running over her own words as she explains that the language may even predate Mesopotamian cuneiform. There was research carried out in the late 1800s by the archaeologist John Howard, who found similar texts in the Welsh foothills and named it Aklo. His theory was that a long-lost race of sub-human beings carved the text.

Folklore will help the PCs tie this theory to tales of the ''wee folk' who were said to inhabit the hills. Perhaps this lost race was the inspiration of the 'fair folk' who those in the area still believe to roam the land even today.

If the strange text from Wilfred's apartment is brought to Catherine, she translates it as the address of the basement where the *Moonwatch* experiments happened close to Lambeth Bridge (Core scene: Experiment Basement).

If Catherine is given the tablet from the Experiment Basement, she spends one interval translating the markings, revealing the text to be a form of ritual spell to create 'sentinels of Arawn'. **Folklore** reveals this to be the Welsh god of the underworld, with a Push noting that Arawn would commence the Wild Hunt, using mortals under his control to drag souls back to his dark domain.

PAN'S GROVE

Scene Type: Core
Bleed: 1
Lead-Ins: Dr Leyland, Experiment Basement
Lead-Outs: Underground Vanishing

The waft of strong myrrh hits the investigators on the way into this cramped occult bookshop. Shelves bulge with all manner of uncanny tomes, from A. E. Waite's *Devil-Worship in France* to *From Matter to Spirit* by Sophia de Morgan. Mary Whitstable is a well put together woman with the crisp accent of the London aristocracy. Her movements are precise as she pores over a leather inventory book, jotting down numbers with a pen. As a saleswoman she immediately begins recommending a host of titles for any investigator that approaches, whether they have spoken or not.

- If asked about Operation *Moonwatch*, Mary is quite candid about her experience. She explains how Leyland, desperate for results, turned away from science and towards sorcery. Mary carried out the ritual of Arawn using the vinum sabbiti as a key ingredient, allowing the subjects to become perfect hunters who would never sleep. She remarks that she took little pleasure in the ritual, having only helped after being given enough money to pay for her premises for the next decade.

- If asked about people turning into oozes, she explains that she had warned Leyland of the future ramifications of the ritual. As with all those that Arawn sends on the Wild Hunt, eventually they are called back to the underworld. She believes that the subjects of *Moonwatch* have reverted to a primordial state and will retreat from the light, going underground where they will continue their master's hunt eternally. It's likely that the creature has made its way into the London Underground (Core scene: Underground Vanishing).

- If given the tablet from the Experiment Basement, she says it's a ritual spell to awaken Arawn's wardens. If the words are spoken in reverse, the spell will also be reversed and the ooze destroyed. The spell is Banish Ancient/Otherworld Being (p.78).

• • •

UNDERGROUND VANISHING

Scene Type: Antagonist Reaction
Lead-Ins: Pan's Grove
Lead-Outs: Tracking the Ooze

Use this scene when you're ready to ramp up the action and have the PCs start investigating the London Underground. Usually this should be after they have discovered the reversal spell or that fire can kill the ooze.

People in the street are starting to panic, talking loudly about an incident at the Leicester Square underground station. Anyone using **Notice** overhears discussions of 'disappearances' and 'a whole carriage'.

Two police officers, one heavy-set and the other rake-thin, stand outside Leicester Square station. They aren't letting people through, which includes the investigators. The broad officer mentions a strange incident on the Northern line. **Charm** or **Negotiate** loosens his tongue slightly, as he whispers in a hushed tone that a carriage was found covered in a black substance and the passengers missing. Passing a Difficulty 4 **Sneaking** or **Athletics** test will get a PC around the police, otherwise a **Charm** or **Negotiate** Push will see them through.

The train stopped at the platform on the Northern line is coated in a thin film of black ooze stretching across the entirety of a carriage. Police officers are standing around looking equal parts stumped and terrified, covering their noses from the acrid stench wafting from the train.

PCs stepping into the carriage see the same ooze coating every surface. **Notice** reveals the ooze has moved away from the carriage lights.

The doors at the trackside appear to have been forced open and a thick layer of ooze leads out of the door and down the tracks into the gloom beyond. Everyone who is heading down the tunnel must succeed a Difficulty 3 **Composure** test or take a Foreboding Place/ Terrible Place Shock card. Following the track leads to Core scene: Tracking the Ooze.

• • •

TRACKING THE OOZE

Scene Type: Core
Lead-Ins: Underground Vanishing
Lead-Outs: The Great Ooze

The sludgy trail continues down the track. A PC succeeding a Difficulty 4 **Sense Trouble** test notices an undulating mass in the near distance and hears a cacophony of muffled animal shrieks. The ooze has absorbed a mass of rats, forming a grotesque rat king. If nobody passes **Sense Trouble**, the rat king (use stats for Primordial Ooze) ambushes the investigators, leading to a fight.

Notice reveals the tracks lead to a large hole in the tunnel side which has clearly been smashed with tremendous force. The stench of rotten eggs emanating from the hole is palpable. The PCs will have to crawl through one at a time. This leads to Core scene: The Great Ooze.

• • •

THE GREAT OOZE

Scene Type: Conclusion
Bleed: 1
Lead-Ins: Tracking the Ooze

The hole in the wall leads to a large pitch-black cavern with a steep 10-foot drop. In the centre of the cavern is an unholy mass of primordial ooze the size of two omnibuses, growling and undulating. **Chemistry** reveals this to be the result of many oozes combining together. Everyone must succeed Difficulty 5 **Composure** tests or take a Cause for Concern/Time to Panic Shock card.

The ooze is crashing against the ceiling causing concrete and stone to cascade.

Dérive reveals that above the ceiling is another underground line, so should the creature destroy it a train would be derailed and plummet to its doom straight into the ooze.

There are several ways the PCs can destroy the mass ooze (p.102):

- By successfully casting the reversal spell from the Aklo tablet. If this happens, the ooze begins to fizz and bubble before seeming to evaporate into the Otherworld.

- By using fire or explosions. **Dérive** shows there are several factories close by where oil barrels can be obtained. The players may come up with other ways to cause an inferno here. However, they must succeed a Difficulty 4 **Athletics** tests or take a Thrown Free of the Explosion/In the Blast Radius Injury card.
- By fighting the creature. That being said, it's not likely the investigators will survive the combat if they take this route, but stranger things have happened.

DENOUEMENT

In all probability the investigators will find a way to destroy the mass ooze and rid the London Underground of the slopping menace once and for all. The police force and members of the public who witnesses the train carriage engulfed in the living sludge will simply attempt to rationalise what they saw. The common explanation in the days following the incident will be a gas leak that had caused hallucinations, and the carriage had never been full of people in the first place. People seem to have a knack for expunging the things from their mind that undermine their world view, so life will rapidly return to normal.

For the investigators, though, it could just be the beginning of a wider mystery. What other secrets do the Aklo texts in the British Museum hold? What may have happened to the archaeologists involved in the dig in the Black Mountains? Where did Mary Whitstable obtain her vinum sabbiti and what does she plan on doing next?

Here are some ideas around where you can take the mystery even further:

- Researchers working on translating a vast array of secret Aklo texts have disappeared. A month later one of their corpses is found by a cave spelunker in the Black Mountains, with strange markings etched in their flesh. The voor have been beckoning the researchers in their dreams to come to the 'Hall of the Mountain King'.
- Residents of a poorhouse are disappearing into the walls, leaving strange fungi where they vanished. Bottles of vinum sabbiti are found hidden in hollowed bricks. A cult of Pan-born operating out of the basement is conducting rituals to turn the building into a beacon to help Pan enter the world.
- Mary Whitstable has vanished while investigating her husband's disappearance, with clues leading to the enigmatic Lost Club. A renowned scientist is experimenting on people, turning them into husks, of which Mary's husband is now one.

CARDS

The following is a list of Injury and Shock cards for use in the game. Each card has a name, injury rules and a degree (Major or Minor). Some cards are not tied to any specific creature or effect listen in the book. Instead, the GM has the option to choose the most relevant Injury or Shock cards for their own mysteries. A downloadable set of these cards can be found at: www.ospreypublishing.com/discover/gaming-resources

INJURY CARDS

Abrasion

Injury: Nonlethal. Roll a die before making an Interpersonal Push. On a 2 or less, you can't make the Push. Discard on a Physical test.
Degree: Minor

Annwn Bite

Injury: -1 to Focus tests. Discard when the hound of Annwn is destroyed or banished.
Degree: Minor

Annwn Paralysis

Injury: -1 to tests. Lose 2 Health. You cannot spend Physical Pushes. Trade for Still Hurting when the hound of Annwn is destroyed or banished.
Degree: Major

Arterial Spray

Injury: If your Health exceeded 4 when you took this Injury, -1 to Physical tests. Otherwise, -2 to Physical tests. Discard as recipient of Difficulty 4 First Aid success.
Degree: Major

A Thorough Thrashing

Injury: -1 to Physical and Focus. On or after two intervals, trade for Black and Blue as recipient of Difficulty 5 First Aid success.
Degree: Major

Automaton Strike

Injury: -1 to Physical and Focus. At end of any interval, roll a die. Even: discard.
Degree: Minor

Badly Beaten

Injury: +2 to Tolls. After two intervals, trade for Black and Blue as recipient of Difficulty 4 First Aid success.
Degree: Major

Badly Hurt

Injury: -1 to Physical and Focus tests.
Degree: Minor

Beak Jabbed

Injury: Roll a die. Even: discard immediately. Odd: lose Health equal to your die roll. Discard after an hour of world time.
Degree: Minor

Beak Stabbed

Injury: Roll a die: lose that number of points from Health, Athletics and Fighting in a distribution of your choice. Discard after an hour of world time.
Degree: Major

Bitten

Injury: -1 to Physical tests. To discard, receive a Difficulty 4 First Aid success then make a Physical test.
Degree: Major

Black and Blue

Injury: +1 to Tolls. Discard when you take a Major Injury.
Degree: Minor

Blow to the Head

Injury: -2 to Sense Trouble tests.
Degree: Minor

Bramble Scratches

Injury: -1 on your next Physical test. Any time after that test, discard with a Difficulty 3 Health success.
Degree: Minor

Breaking Point

Injury: Nonlethal. +2 to Tolls. For the next six hours of world time, other PCs take -2 Composure penalties while in sight of you. After six hours of world time, trade for the Injury card Black and Blue and the Shock card 'They Broke You'.
Degree: Major

Broken Bone

Injury: -2 to all tests. Lose 1 Health each time you make a Physical test. After two Intervals, as recipient of a Difficulty 4 First Aid success, trade for On the Mend.
Degree: Minor

Broken Fingers

Injury: Nonlethal. -2 to non-Presence tests. Penalty drops to -1 as recipient of Difficulty 4 First Aid success. Penalty drops by 1 if in hand at start of session. Discard when penalty equals 0.
Degree: Major

Burned

Injury: -2 to tests (except Preparedness). Trade for Badly Hurt after you fail any test and then receive a Difficulty 5 First Aid success.
Degree: Major

Choked

Injury: Lose 2 Health. +1 to Tolls for rest of the mystery, even after this card is discarded. Discard after one interval.
Degree: Minor

Clawed

Injury: Lose 1 point from all Presence pools. At end of next interval, regain those points and discard this card.
Degree: Minor

Concussed

Injury: You can't make Pushes. Discard after 48 hours of world time.
Degree: Major

Contused

Injury: -1 to Physical tests. Discard on a Physical success.
Degree: Minor

Cough, Choke, Sputter

Injury: -1 to non-Focus tests. Discard at next interval.
Degree: Minor

Crushed

Injury: -2 to Physical tests. Counts as 2 Injury cards. As recipient of Difficulty 5 First Aid success, trade for Black and Blue.
Degree: Major

Crushing Automaton Strike

Injury: -2 to Physical and Focus. After two intervals, trade for Automaton Strike.
Degree: Major

Cudgel Blow

Injury: -1 to Physical tests. At each new interval, roll a die. Odd: -1 to Focus until next interval. Even: discard.
Degree: Minor

Dazed

Injury: -1 to all tests. Discard at end of session.
Degree: Minor

Deadly Venom

Injury: -2 to all tests (except Preparedness). Counts as 2 Injury cards. Spend 3 Health to trade for Badly Hurt. You may do this even if it would otherwise be your Final card.
Degree: Major

Draggy

Injury: Choose one General ability type: Focus, Physical or Presence. -1 to tests of that type. After any failure, discard if you have no other non-Continuity Shock or Injury cards.
Degree: Minor

Drunk

Injury: Nonlethal. -2 to all tests. On a failed test, make a bad, drunk decision. After two hours of world time trade for Tipsy.
Degree: Major

Enveloped

Injury: -2 to Physical and Focus tests. Discard after a Physical success. If still in your hand in four hours of world time, you die.
Degree: Major

Eviscerated

Injury: Counts as 2 Injuries. You can't make Physical tests. After six hours of world time, trade for On the Mend as recipient of Difficulty 6 First Aid success. After 12 hours of world time, Difficulty of that test drops to 4.
Degree: Major

Find the Antidote

Injury: If the mystery ends with this card still in hand, you die. Discard by finding the antidote.
Degree: Major

Flesh Wound

Injury: -1 to non-Focus tests. Trade for Laceration after any non-Focus success.
Degree: Major

Fungal Sproutings

Injury: -1 to Focus and Interpersonal tests. Other PCs around you take -1 Composure. To discard, receive a Difficulty 5 First Aid success.
Degree: Major

Grazed

Injury: -1 to Physical tests. Discard on a Physical success.
Degree: Minor

Hard Landing

Injury: Your next Physical test takes a penalty of -1; then discard.
Degree: Minor

Heavily Sedated

Injury: Roll a die. You remain unconscious for that number of hours of world time. If all characters get this card, they all wake up, confined and in a bad situation. When you wake up, trade for Muzzy Headed.
Degree: Major

Hexed

Injury: Roll a die. Lose Health points equal to the result. If you are then at 0 Health, this becomes a Continuity card. On a success that aids you against a witch, roll a die. Even: discard at end of session.
Degree: Major

Impressive Yet Superficial Cut

Injury: +1 to Presence tests. (Yes, +1.) Spend 2 Health to trade any other non-Continuity Injury you hold for On the Mend. Spend 2 Health to discard.
Degree: Minor

In the Blast Radius

Injury: -2 to Physical tests. Counts as 2 Injury cards. Trade for On the Mend as recipient of Difficulty 6 First Aid success. If still in hand at end of the mystery, trade for Permanent Injury.
Degree: Major

It Looks Worse Than It Is

Injury: Upon seeing you for the first time after the incident that saddled you with this card, any other PC loses 1 Composure. Discard after six hours of world time.
Degree: Minor

It's a Miracle You're Alive

Injury: -1 to Physical tests. After a Physical failure, roll a die. Even: trade for Shock card Rattled.
Degree: Minor

Jarred

Injury: Discard at end of session.
Degree: Minor

Laceration

Injury: When called on to make a Physical test, you may choose to take a -2 penalty on the test and then discard this card.
Degree: Minor

Lingering Cough

Injury: Lose 1 Health point (if available) every time you test a non-Focus ability. At the end of any interval, roll a die. Even: discard.
Degree: Minor

Lungful of Water

Injury: -2 to tests. As immediate recipient of Difficulty 4 First Aid success, or at end of next interval, trade for Cough, Choke, Sputter.
Degree: Major

Massive Injuries

Injury: Counts as 2 Injury cards. Until end of interval, you can't make tests. Thereafter, -2 to Physical and -1 to Focus tests. If the mystery is not over at end of session, trade for On the Mend.
Degree: Major

Monstrous Battering

Injury: -2 to Physical tests. Counts as 2 Injury cards. Trade for On the Mend as recipient of Difficulty 6 First Aid success.
Degree: Major

Mostly Resistant

Injury: You can't spend Health points on tests. At the end of each interval, roll a die. Even: discard.
Degree: Minor

Muzzy Headed

Injury: Lose 1 point from all Presence pools. At end of next interval, regain those points and discard this card.
Degree: Minor

Nodens' Wrath

Injury: Nonlethal. You can't make Pushes. -2 to all tests (except Preparedness). Discard when you leave the boat.
Degree: Major

On the Mend

Injury: -1 to all tests. Trade for Still Hurting on a Physical success.
Degree: Major

Permanent Injury

Injury: Continuity.
Degree: Major

Picked Up and Thrown Hard

Injury: Lose 2 Health and 2 Composure. Discard after half an hour of world time.
Degree: Minor

Precarious Recovery

Injury: -1 to Physical tests. On a Physical failure, roll a die. Odd: trade for the card you traded this card for. Discard on a Physical success with a margin of 3 or more.
Degree: Major

Puncture Wound

Injury: -2 to tests (except Preparedness). Discard as recipient of successful Difficulty 4 First Aid success, or at the end of any interval by spending 2 Health.

Degree: Major

Ravaged by the Elements

Injury: Your Health pool drops to 0. After two hours of table time, roll a die. Even: discard. Odd: trade for Badly Hurt.

Degree: Major

Restrained

Injury: Your foes succeed in rendering you helpless. -1 to Physical tests. When you are no longer helpless and fail a Physical test, discard.

Degree: Major

Ringing Cranium

Injury: -2 to Focus and Presence tests; -1 to Physical tests. After four hours of world time, trade for Blow to the Head.

Degree: Major

Roughed Up

Injury: Lose 1 Composure. Discard after any Physical success, or by spending 1 Athletics.

Degree: Minor

Ructious Innards

Injury: Nonlethal. You must remain within proximity of a water closet. You can't make tests. After six hours of world time, you may make a Difficulty 4 Health test at the beginning of any interval, discarding this card on a success, and losing 3 Health on a failure.

Degree: Major

Scarred Lungs

Injury: Lose 2 Health points and 1 Fighting point (as available) every time you test an ability other than Preparedness. At the end of the mystery, roll a die. On a 1, this becomes a Continuity card.

Degree: Major

Shot

Injury: -2 to Physical tests. Counts as 2 Injury cards. Trade for On the Mend as recipient of Difficulty 6 First Aid success. If still in hand at end of the mystery, you succumb to your injuries and die.

Degree: Major

Singed

Injury: To make an Interpersonal Push you must also spend a Composure point. At any time after the next interval, you may spend 1 Health to discard.

Degree: Minor

Slashed Throat

Injury: You can't take tests or make Pushes, or do anything but lie on the ground bleeding out. As recipient of a Difficulty 5 First Aid success, trade for Stab Wound.

Degree: Major

Snakebit

Injury: Unless you receive a Difficulty 4 First Aid success before end of interval, trade for Deadly Venom.

Degree: Minor

Something in Your Eye

Injury: -3 to Sense Trouble tests, -1 to Physical and Focus tests. Discard on a Sense Trouble, Physical or Focus failure.

Degree: Minor

Stab Wound

Injury: -1 to Physical and Focus. Discard after a Physical or Focus success.

Degree: Minor

Stay by the Water Closet

Injury: Nonlethal. You must remain within proximity of a water closet. -2 to tests. After four hours of world time, you may make a Difficulty 4 Health test at the beginning of any interval, discarding this card on a success.

Degree: Minor

Still Hurting

Injury: Discard on a Physical success with a margin greater than 1.
Degree: Minor

Strange Rash

Injury: -1 to Focus tests. To discard, receive a Difficulty 3 First Aid success.
Degree: Minor

Strong-Armed

Injury: Lose 1 Athletics and 1 Fighting. At next interval, regain those points and discard this card.
Degree: Minor

Sucker Punched

Injury: Lose 2 Health. Roll a die; discard after that number of successes.
Degree: Major

Swallow Your Soul

Injury: Shock: -1 to all tests. Discard once the source of this card is destroyed or banished.
Degree: Minor

Tangled in Thorns

Injury: -2 on Physical tests, -1 on any other tests. After you fail a test and receive a Difficulty 5 First Aid success, trade for Bramble Scratches.
Degree: Major

Throttled

Injury: Lose 2 Health. On or after one interval, trade for Choked as recipient of Difficulty 4 First Aid success.
Degree: Major

Through the Ringer

Injury: +1 to Tolls. Other PCs take -1 Composure penalties while in sight of you. Trade for Black and Blue as recipient of Difficulty 5 First Aid success.
Degree: Minor

Thrown Free of the Explosion

Injury: -1 to Physical tests. When you receive this card, and at every subsequent interval, roll a die. Even: discard.
Degree: Minor

Tipsy

Injury: Nonlethal. -1 to all tests. On a failed test, make a bad, drunk decision. Discard after two hours of world time, or after a test to avoid injury.
Degree: Minor

Turned Ankle

Injury: -2 to Physical tests. Trade for Hard Landing on a Physical failure.
Degree: Major

Warm Blanket Needed

Injury: If you don't get to a warm, dry place by the end of the next interval, you are unable to spend Health points for the following two hours of world time. Discard after two hours of world time.
Degree: Minor

Witch Mark

Injury: Lose 1 Composure. At the end of each interval, roll a die. Odd: lose 1 Composure. Discard on a success that aids you against a witch.
Degree: Minor

Woozy

Injury: Nonlethal. You can't make Pushes. Discard when you leave the boat.
Degree: Minor

You Are Mine

Injury: Shock: -1 to all tests. You can't make Pushes. If in your hand at the start of next session, trade for Shock card Corruption. Discard once the source of this card is destroyed or banished.
Degree: Major

You Should See the Other Fellow

Injury: Nonlethal. You can't make Interpersonal Pushes. Discard after 24 hours of world time, or when you gain another Injury, whichever comes first.

Degree: Minor

SHOCK CARDS

Agitated

Shock: -1 to Presence. When you use an Investigative ability to gain information, roll a die. Even: discard.

Degree: Major

Alarming Vision

Shock: -1 Fighting versus your main foe and its allies. +1 Fighting versus your main foe's rivals. When you gain important information about your main foe, roll a die. Meet or beat the number of Shock and Injury cards you hold to discard.

Degree: Minor

An Image Seared in the Mind

Shock: -1 to Focus. At the end of any interval, make a Difficulty 3 Composure test. **Success:** discard. Becomes a Continuity card if in hand at end of the mystery.

Degree: Major

A Touch of the Shakes

Shock: -1 to Focus. Discard by engaging in a restful activity.

Degree: Minor

Bit of a Sticky Wicket

Shock: -1 to Focus. When you escape your current predicament, discard and roll a die. Odd: gain Shock card Unnerved.

Degree: Major

Brain Twinge

Shock: -1 to Presence tests. Discard when in a Bleed 0 location.

Degree: Minor

Butterflies

Shock: Discard at end of scene.

Degree: Minor

Cause for Concern

Shock: Discard when another PC makes a successful test.

Degree: Minor

Corruption

Shock: Continuity: You can't spend Improvement points. Discard by making a Push and intentionally putting a PC you protect in danger.

Degree: Major

Dread

Shock: -1 to Presence and Focus tests. After any such test, roll a die. Even: trade for Unease.

Degree: Major

Embarrassed

Shock: Nonlethal. -1 to Focus. Discard on a Composure failure.

Degree: Minor

Foreboding Place

Shock: Counts as a Shock card only when you are in the place where you got it.

Degree: Minor

Ghastly Vision

Shock: All PCs take -1 Fighting versus your main foe and its allies. All gain +1 Fighting versus your main foe's rivals. When you aid your main foe, roll a die. Even: discard.
Degree: Major

Glimpsed the Veil

Shock: -1 to Focus tests. Discard when you take a test in a Bleed 2 location.
Degree: Minor

Humiliated

Shock: Nonlethal. -1 to Presence. Discard by winning over a difficult or intimidating witness.
Degree: Major

Ill-Omened

Shock: When your group starts its next fight, its margin before anyone tests Fighting is -2, not the usual 0. Discard when your group loses a fight.
Degree: Major

I Need a Distraction

Shock: -1 to Presence. Discard by taking a risk to indulge a vice.
Degree: Major

Jinx

Shock: Player to your left takes -1 to tests. Discard when that player fails a test.
Degree: Minor

Jitters

Shock: -1 to Focus. Discard by nullifying the consequences of a previous setback.
Degree: Major

Mind's Agony

Shock: -1 Presence for every Shock card you have. You cannot spend Pushes. Trade for Brain Twinge when the force behind the agony is defeated or bound by a spell.
Degree: Major

Oh Dear

Shock: Discard by finding a means of escape.
Degree: Minor

Overstepped Bounds

Shock: -1 on your next Composure test, then discard.
Degree: Minor

Questioning Your Senses

Shock: -1 to Presence. Discard when something you thought might be unreal turns out to be real.
Degree: Major

Rattled

Shock: Your next test takes a -1 penalty. Then discard.
Degree: Minor

Seeing the Great God Pan

Shock: -1 to Composure and Focus tests. Discard when you succeed a test in a Bleed 0 location.
Degree: Major

Shaken

Shock: -1 to Composure tests. After a night's sleep, trade for The Shudders.
Degree: Major

Terrible Place

Shock: -1 to Presence. Discard if, while in the terrible place, you find a core clue or make a Push.
Degree: Major

There's Something About Them

Shock: -1 to Composure tests. When you take another Shock card, spend 1 Composure to discard this one.
Degree: Minor

The Shudders

Shock: Roll a die; lose that number of Composure points, noting the number lost. If your Composure is already 0, trade for Glimpsed the Veil. Discard after a night's sleep. When you discard, roll a die. Even: regain those lost Composure points.
Degree: Minor

Time to Panic

Shock: -1 to Focus tests. Make a tick mark whenever another PC succeeds at a test. Start over on any failure. Discard when you have three tick marks.
Degree: Major

True Form

Shock: After seeing a foe's true form, -1 to Fighting until the end of the mystery. Discard if the foe is defeated.
Degree: Major

Uncertainty

Shock: Discard when something you thought might be unreal turns out to be real.
Degree: Minor

Unease

Shock: Your next Presence or Focus test takes a -1 penalty. Then discard.
Degree: Minor

Unnerved

Shock: Discard by using an Investigative ability to gain information.
Degree: Minor

Wracked by Remorse

Shock: Your next Composure test automatically fails, with a margin of 2. Then discard.
Degree: Minor

THE TERROR BENEATH

Name.. Player..

Background..

Occupation...

Drive..

....

PUSHES (2)

Investigative Abilities

General Abilities

Athletics (Physical)............... ( )
Composure (Presence)........... ( )
Driving (Physical).................... ( )
Fighting (Physical)................... ( )
First Aid (Focus)..................... ( )
Health (Physical).................... ( )
Mechanics (Focus) .... ( )
Preparedness (Presence) .... ( )
Sense Trouble (Presence)....... ( )
Sneaking (Physical) .... ( )

Relationships

→ I Rely On

→ I Protect

THE TERROR BENEATH

ACKNOWLEDGEMENTS

I'd like to thank my partner, Natalie, for her unending patience and her help reading the manuscript. I'd also like to extend my thanks to Robin D. Laws for creating the wickedly effective GUMSHOE system. Finally, I would like to thank Arthur Machen himself for crafting the tales of terror that dug their claws into my imagination and refuse to let go.

CREDITS

ABOUT THE AUTHOR

Scott Malthouse is a roleplaying game designer and folklore enthusiast who was born and bred in Yorkshire, where he currently lives. His work includes the award-winning *Quill* (Best Free Game 2016, Indie RPG Awards), *Romance of the Perilous Land*, *In Darkest Warrens*, and *Unbelievably Simple Roleplaying*.

ABOUT THE ARTIST

Brainbug Design is a 2D conceptual art, illustration, and visual development studio embedded within the entertainment industries. Based in Nottingham, UK, Brainbug was founded in 2018 by industry veterans with over 30 years' combined experience and one singular goal: to burrow deep into intellectual properties to provide the best possible external symbiosis with the host-client! Deeply passionate about world-building and storytelling through the medium of design, Brainbug has collaborated on everything from film and television to giant AAA titles and compact independent video games.